The Virginian Who Might Have Saved Lincoln

Bob O'Connor

By Bob O'Connor

Copyright © 2007 by Bob O'Connor

This is a historical novel. Unlike many novels, all the characters in this book are real characters and the situations are based on fact.

ISBN 0-7414-4031-8

Original cover artwork by
Richard C. Guy
Manassas, Virginia

Published by:

INFIΩITY
PUBLISHING.COM

1094 New DeHaven Street, Suite 100
West Conshohocken, PA 19428-2713
Info@buybooksontheweb.com
www.buybooksontheweb.com
Toll-free (877) BUY BOOK
Local Phone (610) 941-9999
Fax (610) 941-9959

Printed in the United States of America

Printed on Recycled Paper

Published April 2007

Be sure to also read

The Perfect Steel Trap Harpers Ferry 1859
Finalist in the Best Book Awards 2006 by USA Book News

Infinity Publishing
ISBN 0-7414-2944-6
Copyright 2006

Dedication

To my Mother
Wilhelmina Minnihan O'Connor

Thank you, Mom, for all the blessings you have
brought to my life
and for helping mold me into who I am.
I love you.

Capitol Hotel
Richmond, Virginia
April 15, 1865

A loud banging on my hotel room door awakened me from a deep sleep.

"Mr. Lamon. Mr. Lamon. Wake up, sir." The shout was accompanied by more intrusive knocking. It sounded like a battering ram was about to break down my door.

It took me a few seconds to shake the cobwebs from my brain and get my bearings as I struggled to wake up.

"Hold on. I'm coming," I yelled, at the voice in the hallway, while at the same time lighting the lamp and allowing for my feet to become familiar with the cold floor.

"Mr. Lamon. Mr. Lamon. I have an urgent message for you," the voice insisted.

I stood, straightening out my nightshirt, and struggling to find my balance as I stumbled groggily toward the door. "Damn," I thought, "I drank too much last night." I had been known to do that.

The persistent pounding at the door surely must have awakened everyone in the hotel by now.

"What could he possibly want?" I wondered. "The long war has been over for a week. It's the middle of the night. Why can't he leave me alone?"

I opened the door to a young messenger clutching something in his fist.

"Sorry to bother you at this hour, sir, but I have an important message for Ward Hill Lamon. Is that you, sir?" he stammered, out of breath.

"That's me," I said, reaching out to grab the message. "Hold on while I find you a coin for your troubles." I reentered the room, searching for my pants. Finding them on the floor by the bed, I reached into the pocket and secured a silver dollar. That would do nicely for his service. I returned to the door, and flicked the coin to him. "Thanks," I muttered, and closed the door.

Sitting down in the chair by the lamp, I opened the message and read it. I was shocked. Bile rose in my throat as I choked back my anger trying to absorb the catastrophic news. I buried my face in my hands and cried uncontrollably.

Chapter 1

February 11, 1861
Bates Hotel
Indianapolis, Indiana
9:30 pm

The day had been an extremely long one. There was great excitement surrounding our twelve day train excursion, carrying president-elect Abraham Lincoln through the northern states from Springfield, Illinois to his Inauguration in Washington, D.C. We had started our preparations quite early, finally leaving the train station at Springfield at 8:00 this morning.

At each small town and village the train passed through, thousands of supporters yelled and cheered their newly elected Republican president, the "rail splitter" from Illinois.

The emotionally packed day was finally winding down. I personally was looking forward to getting some long-needed rest. But that wasn't to be.

Following his speech in Indianapolis, Mr. Lincoln and I were taken into a hotel room by Mr. Lincoln's friend, Jesse Dubois and some of his cohorts from Illinois. Dubois, who we all knew as "Uncle Jesse," asked me to arrange for a few minutes in private with his group to talk to their friend, the president. I followed Mr. Lincoln into a sitting room on the second floor.

First "Uncle Jesse" talked to Mr. Lincoln, telling him how proud the people of Illinois were of his election. "We expect good things out of you, Abe. You have what it takes to lead this country." And then he added, "Behave yourself like a good boy in the White House." We all laughed. Mr. Dubois took out a knife and cut a lock of Mr. Lincoln's hair. "For posterity," he announced, and the men from Illinois all gave a thumbs up signal.

Mr. Lincoln seemed to be enjoying the attention from his colleagues. The men joked and teased with the future president of the United States as if he were going to be taking on a job they had personally chosen for him. "Don't forget your friends back home," another offered. "We will be watching over your shoulder."

"We know you'll make us proud, Honest Abe," a third one suggested, pounding him on the back for encouragement. "That's why we voted for you."

"We'll be looking forward to hearing about the presidency when you retire back in Springfield, in about four years…err, make that eight years," another laughed.

When that little exchange was over, they said goodbye. I started to leave but as soon as Mr. Lincoln passed out of the door and into the hallway, two men blocked my path to the door. The others surrounded me. They closed the door.

"Mr. Lamon," Mr. Dubois said, very seriously, moving to within just a few inches of my face and looking me straight in the eye. "We entrust the sacred life of Mr. Lincoln to your keeping. If you don't protect it, never return to Illinois, for we will murder you on sight." The others shook their heads in agreement.

It was what I would judge as an amiable threat. I laughed heartily, but none of their expressions wavered at all. They were not kidding. I promptly assured them that I took their threat very seriously. "Gentlemen, no one is going to harm Mr. Lincoln on my watch," I promised. And I meant it.

With that pronouncement, I became Abraham Lincoln's personal bodyguard. You may think, at this point, as a Virginian, I was as unlikely a candidate as anyone for the job. Not so. In fact, I was the perfect person for that appointment.

I had the stature and temperament, the bravado and just enough meanness to take to task anyone who might try to harm the newly elected president. And I was one of the few people in the land who was trusted totally and completely by Mr. Lincoln.

But you couldn't know that without knowing more about me. For that, I need to take you back to the fall of 1849, where my story begins.

Ward Hill Lamon

Chapter 2

One evening a local businessman and I were walking to one of our favorite watering holes in Danville, Illinois when he stopped abruptly to show me someone of interest.

"Look," he said, pointing across the street. "See that beanpole leaning against the lamp post in front of Doc Woodbury's store? That's Abraham Lincoln, the lawyer everyone's been talking about. He will be riding the Eighth Circuit with you. It has been reported that he once walked six miles each way to return a borrowed book when it was due back. I'd have never done that — how about you, Lamon?"

"Actually," I responded quickly, "I admire a man who is willing to make an effort to stand behind his obligations. He is obviously a man with ethics and integrity." It wasn't that I had no ethics or integrity myself, but mine at times were a bit "iffy." Honesty was something I thought was honorable, but it didn't always serve me. I stretched the truth on occasion, and at other times conveniently left out some of the story.

Not long after that, I met John Stuart, a prominent local attorney. Mr. Stuart had been Mr. Lincoln's law partner at one time. Mr. Stuart insisted there was no better lawyer in Illinois than Abraham Lincoln. If I wanted to be a successful lawyer, Mr. Stuart told me, I must meet Mr. Lincoln. He arranged a meeting at the courthouse in Danville on the following Tuesday.

On the day I met Mr. Lincoln, I was all decked out in my usual fashionable attire consisting of a bright green swallow-tailed coat, a ruffled shirt and white neck cloth, with my brown riding pants and field boots. A black stove pipe hat sat high atop my six foot two inch body, making me appear about seven feet tall. My coat hid my two hundred sixty pound solid muscular frame. My outlandish dress was part of the image I was trying to portray; that of a cavalier, swashbuckling, "not to be fooled with" kind of man.

By contrast, Mr. Lincoln was wearing black clothes – the bland, plain clothes he had worn the time I had seen him before. In truth, he reminded me of a praying mantis --- with a stick of a body and two pairs of scrawny appendages attached to the torso. I thought he was one of the oddest looking men I had ever laid eyes on.

His jacket and pants were wrinkled. His coat and trousers weren't nearly long enough to reach his bony wrists and ankles, leaving a two inch gap that remained exposed. Mr. Lincoln was slightly taller than me, and also wore a tall black hat. He was probably twenty years my senior.

Mr. Lincoln greeted me like an old friend. I shook his huge hand enthusiastically, as his long boney fingers engulfed mine. He told me that my cousin, John T. Brown, had warned him that I was coming to Illinois from Virginia.

"Going to try your hand at law?" he asked.

"Yes, sir," I responded, excited that he had already heard of me. "I have been assigned to the Eighth Circuit. I understand you are one of the circuit's most well respected attorneys."

"That depends on who you talk to and what day it is," he said with a chuckle. "When I was a young fellow like you, I was splitting rails. Ever done any hard labor like that, young man?"

"No rail splitting, sir, but I've certainly done my share of manual labor," I added, puffing out my chest with pride.

"Oh yes," he said. "You Virginians shed barrels of perspiration while standing off at a distance and superintending the work your slaves do for you. It is different with us. Here in Illinois, it is every fellow for himself, or the job doesn't get done."

"That wasn't the case in the part of Virginia where I come from, sir," I explained. "My family's farm in the western part of the Commonwealth was quite small -- only about 210 acres. My brothers and I helped our handful of slaves with the work."

"Is that so?" he continued. "That surprises me."

I exaggerated a bit in explaining further. "We worked hard to plant, care for and harvest the field crops, and tend to the orchards and our animals on a daily basis. There was more work than our slaves could finish by themselves. And my family couldn't afford any more slaves."

What I didn't tell him was that work on the farm was surely my least favorite activity, and that I was often missing when the actual hard labor was needed.

Mr. Lincoln laughed as if he didn't believe my story. "What do folks call you?" he asked.

"Hill, sir; that's my middle name," I told him. "It came from my neighbor Colonel Hill, a good friend of my parents."

"And is it pronounced Lay-mon or Lemon?"

"Those family members in the east pronounce it 'Lemon' but my uncles and cousins here in the west say it with the long 'a' sound. I answer to either one," I told him. "It doesn't matter to me how anyone pronounces my last name. It did, however, matter to my cousin, Dr. Theodore who lives here in Danville. He got so tired of people pronouncing his name 'Lemon' that he legally changed the spelling to Lemon, even though his brothers, who live here too, kept their name as Lamon. You probably wouldn't be too surprised to hear that the name changing decreased cousin Theodore's status with the rest of our family."

Mr. Lincoln laughed with me on that one. "I'm Abraham, but folks call me Abe" he responded.

"Mr. Lincoln, sir, with all due respect, I would rather call you Mr. Lincoln, if you don't mind. My mother ingrained in my brain that it was disrespectful to call an adult by his first name," I stated with some embarrassment.

"If you insist, Hill," he said with a little shrug. "You may call me Mr. Lincoln. I'm sure we will meet again when the circuit convenes. Meanwhile, I must be on my way. Good day."

With that, he excused himself politely and he left.

I knew right away I had come out on the short end of our first meeting. That was unusual for me. I normally impressed people the first time around. With me being young and full of vinegar, I thought I knew more than anyone. But Mr. Lincoln had set me back a bit. I went away from that first encounter annoyed that he probably was very unimpressed by this brash young lawyer.

Mr. Stuart prepared me for my position on the Eighth Circuit during the weeks remaining before court convened. He explained to me that "the jurisdiction of the court of the Eighth Judicial Circuit included fourteen Illinois counties, all around and near the state capital in Springfield. The district covered about 120 miles in length and was 160 miles wide."

"Lawyers and judges were scheduled to 'ride the circuit' and travel from town to town," he continued. Courts and trials will convene in the county seat when you arrive."

"When your duties are finished at the first courthouse, you will pack up and ride to the next courthouse. You will complete the entire circuit twice each year; once in the spring and then again in the fall."

I met the others in Decatur at the end of February. Court was to convene in Clinton, the county seat of De Witt County, on the first Monday in March.

The judge and the lawyers proceeded toward Clinton. I had grown up riding horses, so traveling on horseback was not a problem for me. Mr. Lincoln rode right alongside me. He seemed awkward in the saddle, hanging over his horse to the point of almost having his feet touch the ground. He hunched over, probably because it helped him stay balanced in the saddle. But if truth be told, he actually looked a bit more coordinated riding his horse than walking down the street.

Over the first week or so on the circuit, I just basically gawked at Mr. Lincoln like many of the other circuit riders. He was the brunt of many jokes. The other lawyers made fun of his appearance mostly, rolling up their pant legs and jackets and pretending that their clothes were too short, like his.

They poked fun at his scrawny body and his disheveled look. They imitated his awkward walk. Mr. Lincoln seemed

7

to take the ribbing in stride, never letting it bother him.

When I got past all the oddities of his appearance and listened to what Mr. Lincoln had to say in court, I started to formulate a much better impression of him. I began to see traits others missed, because the others had remained stuck on his "less than impressive" appearance. Mr. Lincoln was not someone who was just disheveled and odd looking -- he was a man of substance. His strong character traits set him apart. I admired him for those values. He was straight forward with his comments, and kind to everyone we met.

Mr. Lincoln seemed well educated. His sentences were simple and to the point. He had a firm grip on the law and how it pertained to each case. Clients congregated in his corner and wanted him to defend them, no matter what their difficulties were.

His ability to see through deception played itself out in the courtroom on numerous occasions. He was a man of honor and truth, above all else. The rumor was that no attorney on the circuit was as totally honest as Mr. Lincoln. Without initially taking anyone's word for that, now I was beginning to believe it myself.

It wasn't too long into that first term that I started to like Mr. Lincoln. I desperately needed the legal expertise he was demonstrating, but I also wanted to have some of his character rub off on me. I knew improving my character would be the harder of the two for me to accomplish.

The judge on the Eighth Judicial Circuit was Judge David Davis, or simply "the judge" as the lawyers called him. He traveled right along with us. The judge, all three hundred pounds of him, was a crowd favorite, as he was full of energy and fun to watch.

He also established real early in my career who was boss.

"Lamon, I noticed almost immediately that your attitude needs some adjustment," the judge informed me within the first few weeks of the job. He was referring to the two times he had already interrupted court to reprimand me for talking during a trial. "You need to get used to the fact that I am in charge of the proceedings here. The sooner you learn that, the better we will get along."

It didn't take me too long to figure that out, because day in and day out, Judge Davis was the man sitting on the bench in every courtroom along the circuit. It was very important that I stay on his good side.

The judge also seemed to be in charge of the social arrangements after court had adjourned. He chose where we ate each evening, and even the seating arrangements. "Lamon, you sit there at the end across from Mr. Lincoln," he insisted, as if I were too inexperienced to be able to pick out my own place at the dining table. "Lincoln knows more than anyone what a young lawyer might need to know. Pay attention to him."

A friendship developed between Mr. Lincoln and myself, in my mind, more to my advantage than his. I doubted that he could learn anything good from me. I was quite sure I would learn a great deal from him. But for some unknown reason, he took a liking to me anyway.

I was inquisitive, so I asked Mr. Lincoln lots of questions. "Being a lawyer looks to me like a fine, reputable occupation. Do you find it rewarding after all these years?" I asked when we were getting ready to dine one night in Decatur, Illinois.

"It's a good life if you don't mind always being away from home," he insisted. "I don't see my three boys or my wife, Mary, as much as I used to. But every day is both challenging and rewarding; some more than others. I love the interaction with the people. I am more at home in the courtroom, speaking in front of the judge and jury, that I am anywhere in the world. It comes naturally to me. How do you like being a lawyer?"

"It's growing on me, sir," I ventured. "But it just seems like I've got a lot to learn."

Mr. Lincoln chuckled as if I had told a funny joke. "I thought with you being right out of school, you probably knew everything about being a lawyer already."

"Sometimes I try to give that impression, but between you and me, sir, that's just part of the act," I admitted.

9

"What's taught in school isn't much like what is really happening in the courthouse."

Later, I found that Mr. Lincoln was the best teacher any new lawyer could have. He took me under his wing.

"Keep your eye on the jury," he told me. "They are the pulse of the courtroom. Often you can tell by studying each individual juror which way he is most likely to vote."

"Stay on Judge Davis' good side," he instructed me another time. "When he gets riled up and comes down on you, you'll wish you had stayed in old Virginia."

"The eyes of a client can give away whether he is telling the truth or not. Learn to read their eyes," he explained.

Almost every day I learned something from Mr. Lincoln. And as long as I remained eager and paid attention, he continued to tutor me.

I am not a "sit at my desk" kind of man, so being on the road was always an adventure. The ever-changing environment beat the routine drudgery of an office. Just about the time I got tired of the surroundings in one particular place, it was time to move to the courthouse in the next county.

As soon as court recessed, we made a bee-line to the inn for food, drinks, songs and story telling. It was like a party every single night. Eating and drinking were high on my list of life's most enjoyable pleasures, so I savored the nights.

It was during those evenings that I was constantly trying to impress the judge and the other attorneys. At first I thought that meant I needed to be loud and boisterous to be accepted.

"Bring us enough pitchers of whiskey for all the tables," I would loudly announce upon arrival at the tavern. "They are on me." I thought it best to buy for everyone right from the start to let them know I was one of them.

It probably didn't make much sense to anyone else that the lawyer who had the lowest salary on the circuit was buying the drinks. But considering a pitcher of whiskey cost only ten cents, it wasn't really that expensive. I will admit I was trying to "buy" their friendship. Or perhaps I was trying to prove myself. The phrase "you'll never amount to a hill of beans" resounded often in my head. That's what my mother reminded me whenever I was in trouble at home. It was important to me that I be accepted.

After a while I realized if I had something intelligent to add to the conversation, it got the other attorney's attention faster than if I was just real loud, and I was more apt to attract an audience.

When everyone finished their meal, I pulled out my banjo and sang one silly song after another.

My maternal grandfather, Joel Ward, (from whom I got my first name) had given me the musical instrument around my fifth birthday. When I opened that present, it was the most beautiful thing I had ever seen, even though the banjo had no strings, and it was battered and broken.

But I fixed it up, and Captain Ward, as everyone called him, taught me how to play and sing. There wasn't any time since that birthday when I didn't carry my prized banjo. I was always ready to sing a song or two – with most of my repertoire being minstrel songs and other off-color tunes that made people laugh and encouraged singing along.

You could say I liked the limelight — and I admit it. When I get a little whiskey in me and my confidence kicks in, I am right where I want to be, in the center of attention. My banjo is helping me gain stature on the circuit. At this point, I am much more comfortable playing my banjo than I am being a lawyer.

Early in my days on the Eighth Circuit, I started getting the reputation of loving liquor and consuming it quite frequently. I never lost a dare to see who could drink down his whole pitcher of whiskey first. No matter how many drinking contests I was challenged to, I was always the last man standing. And I was proud of that.

Even after several incidents, I didn't think my drinking was a problem. I believed it was more legend than fact. I didn't want to be known as a drunkard, but I didn't do much to change anyone's opinion either.

I was also gaining the reputation of being a practical

joker. I hid Mr. Lincoln's top hat on several occasions. He got very irritated and let everyone in the tavern know that no one is allowed to touch his stove pipe hat. "I keep important papers in my hat. Please, don't touch it," he insisted. Of course, that doesn't stop me from hiding it. He is so mild mannered that the jokes on him do not cause him undue fuss.

I am less confident in playing tricks on the others. Judge Davis is the most important person on the circuit. It is risky to try to fool him. I noticed his gavel went with him everywhere, even outside the courtroom. He used it to call the court to order or to make his point at the dining table at the Inn. He pounded on everything in site, demanding attention wherever he was. His bang-bang-banging is his signature.

One night when he was ordering another round from the bar, I picked up the gavel from the table and quickly tossed it out the window of the tavern.

When he discovered it was gone, he was madder than an old bear awakened from his winter hibernation. He bang-bang-banged his fist on the table, spilling several drinks from the vibrations, and demanding everyone look around the room for the missing gavel.

While pretending to search the room, I crawled under the table, all the time trying to control my laughter. Others pleaded their innocence. Mr. Lincoln looked at me with that "I know you did it, Hill" kind of look. Shrugging my shoulders and giving him my "Who me?" expression, I excused myself and went outside.

Retrieving the gavel and slipping it into my pocket, I returned with an innocent look. When the judge was ranting and raving to the others, I quietly placed the gavel into his coat pocket and walked back to the other end of the table. Eventually when the ruckus subsided, the gavel was found and all was well. I was not sure if Judge Davis suspected me in that instance or not. He never said. But I was not brave enough to try and play a trick on him again.

Although Mr. Lincoln never joined in helping us drink the pitchers of whiskey (leaving more for the rest of us), he certainly enjoyed the singing and partying. He usually joined and sang along with the chorus of many of my silly songs.

When we exhausted ourselves with the evening activities, we walked to our dormitory room in the various inns. That's where I finally figured out that Mr. Lincoln didn't actually roll his jacket and pants up in a ball like I had suspected from all the wrinkles. He hung them on a chair. But his clothes still looked rumpled in the mornings.

Nearly every night before I went to sleep I lit a cigar. It was a habit I picked up from the older boys in Mill Creek, Virginia where grew up. I sometimes smoked as many as fifteen stogies a day.

"You going to smoke another stinky cigar tonight?" Mr. Lincoln asked, knowing full well the answer. This particular night he was still in the mood for discussion rather than sleep. "When I get home to Springfield, Mary will be able to tell by the cigar stench on my clothes that I have been hanging around close to you," he teased. "I write her often, and you are usually the subject of at least a few sentences. I have mentioned your cigar smoking, your banjo playing, your outlandish dress and your mischievous behavior to her. I told her your cigar smoke sticks like glue to my clothes."

"My wife, Angeline, makes me take my smoking outside the house, and threatens to burn my clothes because they smell so badly," I admitted. "She has to launder them more often than most wives. I know it's because of the smoke from my cigars."

"Tell me about Angeline," Mr. Lincoln insisted.

I hesitated, not really wanting to start that discussion, and then reluctantly explained, "Angeline and I met just before I moved to Illinois. She was from a family with money. I was not. As you might guess, as soon as her father found out my family's financial status, she was banned from seeing me. For some reason, that made her want to be with me even more. We met secretly for several months. The more times we got together, the better we liked each other."

"When I moved to Danville, we courted by mail. I didn't have anyone I knew here except for Bob, a former slave I grew up with, who moved with me. Angeline's letters were comforting and helped push away my loneliness."

"When I went home, we had already planned to be married. But when I asked her father for Angeline's hand, he was furious. He would not allow her to marry me. He forbid it, in fact. We ran off the next morning and got married anyway. And then I brought her and her servant girl, Topsey, to Danville."

"Tell me more about your wife," I insisted, in response to his questions for me.

Mr. Lincoln hesitated too, as if weighing the words before he answered. "Mary's a good woman and a good mother to our boys," he explained. "But I am very difficult to live with. She lets me know how difficult I am on a regular basis."

"I know the feeling, sir," I offered. "I know it well."

Lamon and Lincoln
Lloyd Ostendorf – used by permission

Chapter 3

My keen powers of observation helped me to formulate strategies I needed to become an effective lawyer. I sat in the front row of each trial, watching and listening intently to the judge, the witnesses, the juries and the other attorneys. I took notes on which cases were won and lost, which points seemed to be favorable to the judge and juries, and what persuasive measures freed the defendants of their charges. The more I observed the actions in the courtroom, the more I noticed that one man stood out. Mr. Lincoln towered over all the rest, not only in stature, but in professional ability too.

His arguments in court made more sense than those of any other lawyer. Even with all the background information I researched for him, often his arguments came from other sources. He was quick to use an example from the Bible or from some point he remembered from history. And he was usually right on target, conjuring up an idea or two that "sold" his argument to the judge or jury.

He seemed well educated to me. But when I asked him about it, I was surprised.

"I fooled you on that count, Hill," he confessed, smiling. "I have just been to school 'by the littles' — having had less than a year of formal education. What I know I have picked up along the way out of necessity. No one in my early days excited in me the ambition for education."

I was quite astonished. "I never would have guessed," I admitted, shaking my head in disbelief. "You are perhaps the best example of a self-made man I know. You are smarter than all the other lawyers, and some of them have graduated from established universities."

Mr. Lincoln could be solemn and quiet at one point, and then quickly turn on the enthusiasm when arguing his point before the court. There didn't seem to be any middle ground.

During his quiet times, it was almost like Mr. Lincoln

turned everything else off and went into the world of his own mind. He became morose and perhaps even melancholy. I got the impression during those times that he didn't want anyone to talk to him. When I was around and he got real silent, I just waited.

By contrast, when he was deep into his arguments in court, he was sharp and alert. He seemed to get energized just at the right moment. He could go back and forth from one mood to the next, like a chameleon changing colors with the background.

Mr. Lincoln often sought me out to ask my opinion of the cases he was working on. He prodded and poked at me, trying to figure out where I stood on some of the issues. I was impressed that he listened intently even when I mumbled and rambled, trying for the life of me to establish some actual support for my own beliefs.

I remember our first conversation about a particular trial like it was yesterday. "Hill," he said with a grin, motioning me to sit at the table in the hallway outside the courtroom. "Did you notice Attorney Leonard Swett getting lambasted by Judge Davis in that last case this afternoon?"

"Definitely, Mr. Lincoln," I offered, pulling up a chair at the end of the table next to him. "I was sure glad the judge wasn't yelling like that at me. Mr. Swett, it seems, was rather insulting to Judge Davis when the judge failed to sustain his motion. I certainly thought the judge had a right to come down on him as hard as he did. Do you think he'll rescind the contempt citation he issued against Mr. Swett when we get back in court tomorrow?"

"I think he'll keep Mr. Swett hanging just a little longer for affect. It's a new term of the court, and it's early," Mr. Lincoln said, setting his top hat on the floor between us and combing his hair with his fingers. "I think the judge wanted to let those of you who are green around the edges know who is in charge here. Any questions?"

"No sir," I answered. "I got the message. I understand the need to set the early precedent. I just feel sorry for Mr. Swett."

"Don't. He's a veteran who knows better. You, my friend, being new at this, would have had an excuse," he added, with a laugh.

Later that evening, Mr. Lincoln asked me about another court case from the docket we had just finished. "What did you think of that divorce case verdict this morning, Hill?" he asked, referring to a case he had lost. His client was a lady who had asked the court to grant her a divorce due to neglect and abandonment by her husband.

"Seemed to me the judge entirely missed the point that you were trying to make," I argued. "All of your witnesses told of her husband's escapades with several other women when his wife thought he should have been home with her. I was dumbfounded when Judge Davis found the man innocent of the charges. What's your take on it, sir?"

"Good observations, Hill. Although my witnesses were a little shaky on their facts, it was obvious the husband was paying attention to ladies other than his wife. I honestly thought the judge would rule in her favor. Judge Davis' decision will just encourage the man to do more of the same, now that he knows he can get away with it."

"If she'd have just boxed her husband's ears, and not bothered to bring the issue to court," I suggested, "she would have fared better. I have heard of that happening in Virginia."

"I don't think my Mary would tolerate me paying attention to another woman like that," Mr. Lincoln said, shaking his head. "I would be mighty frightened of what she might do to me if she caught me. What would your wife do, Hill?"

"Unfortunately, I think Angeline has a convincing case of my neglect she could pursue right now," I admitted with some embarrassment. "Angeline thinks I am married to my job. She might say I abandon her while I'm on the circuit. And it would be hard to defend myself if she brought her case to this court."

"Actually, if the truth be known," I admitted painfully, "there are days I don't feel married. My wife and I are not close physically or connected in any way, except for a legal marriage certificate. We rarely speak, and hardly ever discuss anything of substance. I doubt if I could tell you her stance on any subject. If anyone asks her if it is enjoyable to be married to me, I'm sure she would say 'No' without even thinking about it. I often wonder if I shouldn't have married my first love, Mollie Pultz, who I left behind in Virginia."

"Who's this Mollie?" he insisted.

"A classmate from school. A friend. A long-time companion who I really miss."

He waited patiently, but I was not willing to go any further.

"Your descriptions about her were quite short and choppy, like you don't want to let me in on your secret."

"Sometimes you scare me, sir, because you can see right through me. I haven't told anyone about her, including Angeline," I admitted.

"What happened to her?" Mr. Lincoln asked.

"Mollie Pultz wanted badly to be Mrs. Ward Hill Lamon. When I left for Illinois, she thought I would be taking her with me. When I told her I was leaving without her, things got ugly. In fact, she called me names that even made my face red, if you can believe that. Most of those words would have gotten her the lye soap treatment, to wash out her mouth. I said some things I have long regretted. I can't take them back now. But I do think about her often and wonder how things might have been different."

"I was in love some years ago too," Mr. Lincoln offered. He spoke as if there were still some pain. "Anne Rutledge. She was engaged to a man who left the area and promised to come back for her. Anne waited several years. By then, she and I talked about getting married. She was determined to do the honorable thing, and tell the other man face-to-face that she wanted to break her engagement when he returned. My friend, Anne, died suddenly before she was able to tell him."

He got real quiet, hanging his head. I was surprised and shocked. But I didn't say anything. I waited.

"I have not told many people about her," Mr. Lincoln

admitted. "Please don't say anything. Mary does not know and would surely not understand. I too wonder how things might have been different."

"I will not tell a soul," I assured him. "I can be trusted. Your secret is safe with me."

I was excited that Mr. Lincoln had trusted me as a friend. I would not let him down on that score.

Mr. Lincoln and I spoke often, away from the others, on matters of law but also on a variety of other topics.

I tried to use my loud demeanor and overzealous spirit to substitute for lack of any stand on the issues. Being brash and bold, I often forced my arguments without thinking them through. I was more concerned with being heard than with choosing sides. I often won arguments by intimidation.

But Mr. Lincoln wouldn't accept that from me. He forced me to ask myself some serious questions and come up with answers that defended my positions.

"Come on, Hill," he insisted. "You must be on one side or the other — you cannot be like the ox who jumped halfway over the fence. You have to take a stand. It matters not what your stand is. And it doesn't matter how loud you announce your position. But it surely matters that you have a view and can defend it."

He wanted to know what my feelings in general were about women. He admitted, "Although I am married, I have no idea how women work, what they want, or why they do what they do. I am even afraid to talk to most ladies, though I try at least to be polite in my shyness."

"My wife, Mary," he continued, looking a bit squeamish with the subject matter, "is insanely jealous even when I stand next to another woman. She's strong willed and has a temper not to be fooled with. I tiptoe around the house on days when she isn't feeling well. But she need not worry about my interest in other ladies. If she knew how scared I felt inside around any lady, she would not be concerned. I am just trying to make her happy and content, but I may be failing at both."

"I didn't think, sir, that you were afraid of anyone," I

said, quite surprised at his admission, and smiling at the image of Mr. Lincoln tiptoeing around his own house. "Now you tell me that you are afraid of women. I find that quite comical."

"Oh, I wasn't always afraid of them – it's something I have developed over the years," Mr. Lincoln confided, blushing as he spoke. "In fact, after Anne Rutledge's death, I pretty much thought that I would not ever marry," he continued. "I was not sure I could ever be satisfied with anyone who would be foolish enough to choose me."

I was, on the other hand, comfortable talking about the ladies. "I too have little understanding of women," I admitted, "but I love being around them. Their presence comforts me. But having said that, I certainly have little knowledge I can impart to you as to what makes ladies do the things they do," I continued, noticing that he was now smiling at my handling of the subject. "I would rather be with them than without them. I enjoy most of the women I know. But my wife would probably tell you that she is the exception."

Mr. Lincoln also admitted that he knew little about proper etiquette and decorum. "Mrs. Lincoln scolds me because I don't even know how to bow," he offered uncomfortably. "She has threatened to hire someone to teach me how to doff my hat," he said, tipping his hat in such an awkward manner that he almost lost his grip of it.

"I see that you might need some lessons," I added, chuckling out loud and agreeing with her assessment of his less than spectacular doffing technique. I tipped my own hat expertly in response. He nodded his approval.

"I do know proper manners, though I am not always one to show that knowledge," I continued brashly. "I am sure loud belching after meals is not on the list of acceptable etiquette. You, sir, are welcome to copy some of my manners, as long as you choose wisely what you are copying."

I think he thought that was quite an outrageous sugges-tion.

20

Mr. Lincoln professed an interest in politics. He had been a Congressman in Washington but had decided not to run for re-election. "As a new legislator, I thought I could affect the legislative process. I was mistaken," he explained. "I returned to the circuit instead. Others are prodding me to run for elective office again, but I am not certain I am suited for another venture in that arena."

He asked me about my thoughts on politics. I didn't have much to say on that subject.

"There you go again," Mr. Lincoln said, shaking his head from side to side. "Having no opinion is not acceptable. You don't have to agree with anyone, but you must have your arguments well prepared. And you can certainly change sides if you see that the other viewpoint is stronger. Having no thoughts on the subject doesn't serve you."

"Take your friend, Bob, for instance," he continued. "Did you ever have a conversation with him about slavery? Did he like being a slave? How does he feel now that he is a free man?"

"I think he liked being a slave," I told Mr. Lincoln, realizing while I was talking that I had not thought about his situation the entire time I had known Bob. "We treated him kindly on our small Virginia farm. He and the other coloreds were considered part of our family. I never saw them beaten though I have heard of instances that some other slaves in the region had been treated cruelly. I don't think he had any complaints. But I certainly never discussed it with him."

"So, Hill," Mr. Lincoln wondered aloud. "Do you think you would have liked to have been a slave?"

"I don't think I would have minded it," I said with some assuredness.

"Go talk to Bob, and then come back and give me a report," Mr. Lincoln suggested. "And then we will discuss the matter further."

And so I did. The next time the circuit schedule took us to Danville, I sat down with Bob. We were about the same age. Growing up in Virginia, I spent more time with him than I did with my own brothers and sisters. Bob was the closest friend I had. He was loyal and trustworthy on all counts. As my life-long friend, he understood me far better than Angeline, and that drew me closer to him.

At Mr. Lincoln's suggestion, I asked Bob about his feelings on the subject of slavery.

"What you askin me that for, Massa Hill?" Bob asked.

"I just thought it was about time I asked you what you thought about being a slave, after all these years."

"Massa Hill," Bob explained slowly, as if he was trying to decide what to tell me. "No disrespect for your father or your family. I love them all. They are my only family. There ain't nothin I wouldn't do for you. But how'd you like to be just property — like the chickens and the hogs? How'd you like to have no rights you white folk had to respect?" he asked. Without letting me answer, he went on. "How'd you like to be sold away from the rest of your family at any time, not being able to stay together, and never hearin from your wife or youngins again." I listened intently and was surprised how angry he was starting to sound.

"Wait a minute, my friend," I interrupted, holding up my hand. "My family treated you and the other slaves real good. You had a place to live and were fed like family. Being a slave at the Lamon farm was no worse than being one of the Lamon children. I didn't have anything to do with your family being sold away. You were never beaten. I…"

"Dammit, Hill," he fumed. "You asked me 'bout my thoughts. I've been saving them up for a long time 'cause no one has ever wanted to hear me. So just shut that big mouth of yours for once and listen to what I want to say."

He had never talked to me with such disrespect and it made me angry. Without thinking, I grabbed Bob. He started swinging at me. I dwarfed him in size and always won when we scuffled playfully. This time he wasn't playing. He scrapped and punched and tore at me like a cornered animal fighting for his life. "Don't you ever tell me to quiet my mouth, boy. I'll teach you who is in charge around here," I shouted, trying to get him under control. But he beat on me like an old drum, clawing, scraping, and tearing my clothes.

22

He pulled loose, like he was going to run off, but instead came right back at me with his arms flying in all directions at once. His quickness surprised me. I was just trying to subdue him, not hurt him, but he was fighting fiercer than a starving tiger. I lost my footing and fell on my back. He was on top of me before I knew it, hitting me with both fists as the same time. I put my hands up to block his punches, while at the same time trying to get back on my feet. His fists found pay dirt more than once, connecting with my face and causing my nose to bleed.

"Get off me. I own you and you will do what I tell you," I yelled. The second that expression came out of my mouth, I regretted it.

"See what I mean. You don't own me. Dammit, Massa Hill, did you forget that you freed me when we crossed into that free state of Ohio? So what are you going to do if I tell you to shut that big mouth of yours. You gonna beat me to within an inch of my life and teach me what I was missin all those years at your daddy's farm? You gonna turn me in for a reward to a slave catcher? You gonna whip me and starve me until I die a slow death? Just what you gonna do now that you suddenly remember that you don't own me any more?"

"Oh God, Bob. I am so sorry. And stupid. I am feeling terminally stupid right now." I hung my head. I couldn't look at him. I was embarrassed with my behavior. This was my friend who I had asked about his feelings. And then I didn't like what he had to say. I had acted no better than the plantation owners who beat their slaves. I felt awful.

I took some deep breaths. I held out my hand as a truce. He shook it. "God, I am sorry, my friend. I was totally wrong. I have no right to address you as 'boy' or to try to exert any more authority over you than I would any other man. I have never been sorrier in my life than I am now."

He was watching me closely as he brushed himself off. Even if I had actually won the battle, I had definitely lost the war. "Yes, I want to hear you out. I will close my big huge mouth and listen to what you have to say. Please help me to understand what being a slave was like."

"We go back a long ways, Massa Hill. I know you didn't mean nothin bad, just like I didn't mean nothin bad by tellin you to shut your mouth and listen. I wouldn't hurt you, ever, but there for a minute I wanted to kill you. I'm sorry too. I guess we never talked about slavery because we was too busy fishin and swimmin and ridin horses. So how would you have known?"

We had both calmed down a bit by now. I thought about what he had said, trying to see his side. He was right. I had been blinded by the circumstances, probably because I didn't want to see his problem. "I understand how you could be angry with me for not realizing your situation," I admitted. "But please, will you explain further?"

"Well, Massa Hill," Bob went on. "It's like this. Seems to me that the country sees color differently than I do. They think white is good, and black is bad. It ain't that simple. Did you ever know a bad white man? I seen lots of them. I'd bet you have too. Have you ever seen a good black man? I seen a few of them too. How 'bout you? Did you ever know a white man to lie and cheat? Of course you have. Did you ever know black man to lie and cheat? You have seen that too. So, I ask you. What's the color of your skin got to do with all that?"

Bob was right and I admitted it. But he wasn't finished.

"So Massa Hill. I am property and you are human. Does that make sense to you? You never offered to trade places. If I could read and write, I'd be just as smart as you – but I ain't allowed to be ejucated. I just gotta lay down and 'cept whatever you white folks say. You think them rules are fair?"

"Bob, as smart as you think I am I had no idea that you had these feelings. And you are right in what you are saying," I told him as if some understanding was finally creeping into my brain. "In fact, I can't think of anything you just explained that I don't agree with. How could I have been such friends with you and not noticed?"

"Massa Hill," Bob explained. "I am thinkin you seen it all along, but you are not willin to admit it 'cause it is just the way things are. Nobody's gonna do nothin about it. Ain't ever gonna change. Look right here where we live in Illinois, a free state. The folks here look at me thinkin I am still a slave – but I'm free. None of you know what to do with me. So I'm free — but I cannot vote. I cannot go to school. I kin have a job and be paid, but there's no white folk wantin to hire me. I kin buy land, but I ain't got no job and I ain't got no money. So how's I gonna ever buy land? I ain't seen a whole lot of difference between bein a slave and bein free. You, Massa Hill, is the only one who treats me like a friend. You are the only one who don't see me as black – you have gotten past that."

"Bob, you are right again," I admitted. "I never looked at you as black and me as white. We have always just been friends. It's not about your color. I trust you, I like you, and I enjoy your company. I know lots of white folks I don't like, and I don't trust, and I wouldn't want to spend time with."

I was enlightened and surprised. I wondered what Mr. Lincoln was up to when he asked me to find out how Bob felt about slavery.

When we returned to the next session on the circuit, Mr. Lincoln and I had time to talk about slavery again. He was delighted that I had learned so much.

"So, Hill, if someone asked you before you talked to Bob if you were for slavery or against slavery, what would you have told them?"

"For slavery sir, without question," I quickly answered.

"And today, are you for slavery or against?" Mr. Lincoln asked with a smile.

"Against, sir," I stated assuredly.

"And can you defend your stand?" he wanted to know.

"Yes sir. I know my arguments and am ready to defend my position," I announced proudly. "I made a fool of myself along the way, sir, acting like a damn angry slave owner who was trying to control his slave. But Bob straightened me out, and bloodied my nose in the process."

Mr. Lincoln laughed with me as I recounted my confrontation with Bob, and how embarrassed I had been to put myself it that position. But he was also impressed as to how much I had learned from Bob. He congratulated me on my new found knowledge.

"I too am against slavery, Hill," Mr. Lincoln explained. "As a youngster I saw slaves being sold at auction in New Orleans. That scene sort of stretched my eyes and ears, and stretched me all over inside. I have never been the same. Watching that slave trader has haunted me ever since. As a legislator in Washington, I introduced a bill to eliminate slavery in the District of Columbia. Although it was defeated, I still think slavery should have been abolished in Washington."

He continued on with the same resolve he usually displayed in the courtroom. "The system of slavery is unjust and a disgrace for a country founded on the principles that all men are created equal."

"Thank you for helping to open my eyes, sir."

"You have two eyes and two ears. And only one mouth. Use them wisely. The mouth should only be used about half the time as the eyes and ears," Mr. Lincoln instructed me.

"As you know sir," I acknowledged, "I usually use my mouth much more than the other two. I just wish you would have told me that before I talked to Bob."

"I know that your mouth is a source of many of your problems, Hill," he laughed.

"Remember the judge halting those trials to get you to stop talking? And your drinking just makes your mouth work even more than its fair share. I realize it will not be easy for you to make the change to listening more and talking less.

But I do think if you follow that advice, you might just turn out to be a better man."

The lesson about slavery and the one concerning using my mouth, eyes and ears, were gifts from Mr. Lincoln. I was sure those lessons would serve me well. I did not think, however, cutting the use of my mouth in half was going to occur quickly. My mouth had been operating non-stop for all these years, and to change that overnight would be a challenge for me.

I realized early on that Mr. Lincoln took particular pleasure in showing me that I still had plenty to learn. "Hill, life presents you with lessons each and every day," he taught me. "You just have to allow yourself to be aware and to learn from them."

After a while, I started to notice more things happening around me. They had probably always been there, but Mr. Lincoln's insistence that I be more aware, helped me to "see" them.

I noticed more and more of the value of Bob's friendship. Actually I think our confrontation had drawn us closer. I watched as others dealt with Bob in my presence. He was right. Bob was not being treated the same as me even when I was standing right there next to him. I wondered how people treated him when I was not around. And I knew the special treatment he was getting was only because of his skin color. And that he was not being treated fairly.

I was also beginning to see what a good influence Mr. Lincoln was becoming in my life. My need to swear had diminished. I was drinking less. I was not as likely to voice my opinions without first considering what I had to say on that particular subject. I hadn't been in a fist fight lately. And those were all good things.

I appreciated what I was learning from Mr. Lincoln. Before becoming friends with him, I didn't think there was anything else I needed to know. And it was not easy for me to admit at this point in my life that I could improve any.

I explained further to Mr. Lincoln, pointing to my head. "Any lessons will have to sink into this thick cranial cavity slowly. The ingrained ideas that have been planted there for a long time will fight being replaced with new ideas. So if you will, sir, please be patient with me."

Chapter 4

One day before court convened, a man insulted a lady who I had been talking to on the courthouse steps. I stood up for her and within a few seconds, found myself defending her with my fists – hitting first, without thinking about the consequences. I ended up rolling all the way down the stairs, tumbling down with the perpetrator. Since I had about a hundred pounds on him, he suffered the brunt of the situation.

I picked myself up and received thanks from the grateful lady. I brushed off my clothes, and entered the courtroom a bit more disheveled than usual and out of breath, barely in time for the opening session.

When court convened, I had to deliver my remarks in front of the bench. My presentation caused quite a spectacle for those watching. It was obvious to them that I was literally hanging out in the back of my pants, though I had not notice that my trousers had been torn in the fight.

A fellow attorney decided to make a big fuss about it, passing a subscription to the others in the courtroom. At the recess, he spoke eloquently about how I had defended the lady's honor. In the ensuing scuffle, I had torn my clothing. He said everyone owned me a debt of gratitude for what I had done. He asked for donations to purchase pantaloons for me, indicating that I was "a poor but worthy young man." He actually collected a small sum of money.

When the petition reached Mr. Lincoln, he wrote, "I can contribute nothing to the end in view" next to his name.

Everyone certainly made me the joke of the day, but Mr. Lincoln's comment got the biggest laugh.

After that incident, Mr. Lincoln told me as we were walking back to the Inn, of his physical prowess in growing up. "Hill, like you, I let my fists do my early talking for me. Boys would come from miles around to fight – trying to take away my crown as champion of the whole area. I'm pretty sure I could button your ears back and swallow you whole too."

I was surprised. "You, the skinniest man alive," I challenged, "were a champion fighter? You are the most honest man I have ever known. But I think you are lying this time."

He suggested we arm wrestle in the tavern so he could prove himself. I was open to that. No one had ever beaten me in competition. I knew I would win this match too.

I followed him into the saloon. We sat down across from each other, positioned our arms and locked hands. A crowd gathered around to watch and place bets on the match. Before I could say "one, two three, go", he had pinned my arm on the table.

"No fair. I wasn't ready," I announced loudly, hoping someone in the tavern would realize that I had not actually lost but had been tricked. "That little stunt, Mr. Lincoln, proved nothing."

"Oh, all right," Mr. Lincoln agreed. "In a fight, there are no rules. You have to be ready at anytime. In this case, however, I will give you another chance. You say when."

We reset our arms and hands. I was confident to the point of being cocky. It would be no contest. He nodded to me to give the signal. I shouted, "Begin" and we started on much more even terms. This time I put up good resistance for about three seconds and then found my arm lying prone on the table again. The men watching gave Mr. Lincoln a round of applause.

I was right. It was no contest. I thought to ask for the best two out of three, but my arm was in so much pain, I thought the better of it. I conceded he would have won all three. He could have broken my arm off if he wanted to. He was stronger than any man I had known, in spite of his scrawniness. I was both shocked and impressed.

"Damn," I said. "That rail splitting time you bragged about was time well spent. I would never have thought you were so strong. I am very embarrassed that I thought you were lying. I should have known better. I apologize that I didn't believe you, sir."

Mr. Lincoln just smiled and suggested "others had made that same mistake, underestimating my strength. They too had paid the price."

Just as quickly, he put that episode behind us, and reminded me that now he talked his way out of sticky situations, instead of fighting. He suggested that I might adopt a similar policy. I told him I would think on that matter.

In the courtroom, Mr. Lincoln was the most entertaining person the circuit had. All the eyes in the courtroom were on him when it was his turn. As he climbed slowly out of his chair, unwinding those long arms and legs and taking that first step toward the witness, I think the people in the courtroom were wondering if he would walk forward or fall on his face.

He used silence to perfection. The longer he waited to ask a question or paused in his remarks to the jury, the more the people in the courtroom listened in anticipation. He was like the conductor, timing his delivery and playing his audience like the maestro of a fine orchestra.

Animation seemed a natural part of Mr. Lincoln, as he waved his long arms to pull an imaginary question out of thin air, spun around quickly to make a point, or scratched his head and acted like he was puzzled by the testimony. He would wave a petition back and forth in front of the jury to make sure they focused on the point that he was making. Mr. Lincoln dramatically dug deep into his tall hat to extract a document he wanted to introduce to the court. He often made the witness nervous by pacing back and forth without saying anything at all for what seemed to be interminably long periods of time.

He used these antics to his advantage. I was not sure whether his gestures were rehearsed or natural.

And it didn't matter if he was talking to a crowd, pleading his case in front of the judge or jury, or just standing outside. People were fascinated to be around Mr.

Lincoln. And I was certainly one of the most ardent of his supporters.

I continued to study law by taking on assignments to help the more established lawyers gather information for their trials. I stayed into the night on many occasions, going through the law library to find documentation I needed for their cases. I made some mistakes as I was learning how to match the legal opinions with the case at hand. Mr. Lincoln was not always patient when I botched the findings for one of his clients.

"Hill," he scolded me one night. "The law case you brought to me today on the trespassing incident was not helpful in proving my client innocent. What were you thinking? You were careless and lazy. You can do better than this."

I knew he was right but with my stubbornness, I was loath to admit it. It felt like I got caught stealing and it didn't sit well with me. It reminded me of all the times I sat in the corner wearing the dunce cap at Mill Creek School. I vowed silently to be more careful. I would spend even more time researching the law books even if I had to burn the midnight oil to get it right. I hung my head in embarrassment and was determined to sulk the rest of the evening. But Mr. Lincoln would have none of that.

"I don't want you sulking around either. You made a mistake. Admit it and then don't do it again." And with that, he didn't mention it any further. And I worked even harder in the library to make sure the information I was gathering fit the case at hand.

I put in extra hours to try to improve my research techniques and I was getting better as time passed. My errors were less frequent, but I still had an occasional lapse. I was sure I quoted the proper law case to use in a land dispute. Mr. Lincoln lost the case. "Hill," he said when he caught up with me. "The judge was familiar with the case you cited, and said the reference actually helped solidify the prosecution's case against my client. You are supposed to be helping me defend, not aiding the prosecution, which is akin to joining the enemy."

I decided not to be defensive this time as I remembered he didn't find that acceptable behavior on my part. "Sorry, Mr. Lincoln. I would never do anything intentionally to make you look foolish. In fact, I will go over that case again before I finish my work for tonight, just to make sure I see what my error was."

Even in his disappointment with me when I made a mistake, he gave me another lesson. "If I didn't like you, Hill," he admitted, "I wouldn't be trying to help you improve yourself."

Dr. William Fithian, Lamon and Lincoln
Danville, Illinois
Lloyd Ostendorf – used by permission

Chapter 5

One night in Danville, I got a little crazy at the local tavern. The owner, Jacob Schatz, a short quiet man who happened to be tending the bar, decided to confront me when I asked to have him carry my purchases on credit. "Lamon, as you know, you must pay cash for your whiskey. You have not established credit here."

"I am a local businessman of some note, and a lawyer," I insisted, "who is allowed to pay by credit in every other tavern in Danville. What makes this place so special that I can't have a credit account?"

"You know the rules here, Lamon, as well as anyone," Schatz argued. "Don't cause me any more trouble." The other patrons gathered round to listen to our dispute.

My friend, Chickamauga Jim, was standing alongside of me, and enthusiastically supporting my logic. Schatz had other ideas. "Lamon," he shouted, "you can take your business elsewhere anytime you like, but you are getting no credit from me."

I guess he thought I would just pick up and leave. By that time, because I had drawn a crowd, if I left I would lose face. I had to make a stand. And I did. I couldn't believe with my good name, I didn't have enough respect to be able to sign for my drinks.

I became angry at Schatz's stubbornness. "I think instead of leaving, Mr. Schatz, I will teach you a lesson you won't soon forget," I said, moving closer and hovering over him. As Jim held Schatz's arms back, I pummeled him with both my fists until he could not stand any more. Jim let go and Schatz fell to the ground. The man didn't move. I actually feared at first that I had killed him. But soon he was moaning and groaning. He demanded I leave his establishment.

Instead, I went behind the bar, stepping over him, and poured several more pitchers. The entire entourage began toasting my great accomplishments. The celebration was short lived. The constable arrived and took both Jim and myself into custody. We spent the night in jail.

By morning, Schatz filed formal charges against James "Chickamauga Jim" Kilpatrick and myself for disorderly conduct.

Mr. Lincoln agreed reluctantly to defend us, though he suggested that our crime was indefensible. He urged me to plead guilty. He felt I could get off with a minimal fine and carry on without damaging my career.

But no. I wanted to fight the charges. I wanted Schatz's neck. How dare the man. Didn't Schatz know who I was? "Let's take this to court, Mr. Lincoln," I insisted. "I want his tavern license revoked for at least a month. That will teach him to mess with Ward Hill Lamon."

"No, Hill," Mr. Lincoln insisted, grabbing my arm. He talked to me calmly, but shook his long finger in my face. I found both his calmness and his shaking finger very annoying. "You have to pick your fights based on the principle involved. This is not an important issue. Just plead guilty on this matter and forget about it. A jury might find you guilty. Then you, Mr. 'know it all' Attorney, will be suspended from practice. That'll be a fine mess even I won't be able to get you out of."

I started to defend myself with my side of the story, but Mr. Lincoln was not through with me quite yet. "Your behavior as a lawyer has to be above reproach at all times, not just when it is convenient for you," he continued, getting louder with each point of his argument, and in his best courtroom decorum. "I have tried to impress on you that attorneys have a higher moral standard than ordinary fellows, like Jim. Nowhere in our code does it give you the authority to beat someone to a pulp just because you think you are right. Do you think the law doesn't apply to you, you stubborn fool?"

I cursed under my breath and fought him for an hour or so, demanding I was right. And Kilpatrick agreed with me, which encouraged me further. I stomped around the room, kicking an imaginary Schatz with my boots as if he were still lying on the floor. I was fuming, and for good reason. This time I was right.

I clenched my fists and shadow boxed. I swore under my breath, using most of those words I had been taught by the older boys but I hadn't been able to use as a lawyer. I was ready to fight again.

"Jim and I will go to trial and take our chances, sir," I said, pretty sure of myself. "And if you don't want to defend us, we will find someone else."

Mr. Lincoln laughed and shook his head back and forth. That annoyed me even further. And then he added insult to injury, suggesting, "Jim's case doesn't matter a lick. He is not a lawyer. He would not get suspended from law practice and reprimanded like you will, Hill."

I didn't want to let go. I knew Mr. Lincoln was right. But I was a proud, pig-headed and stubborn man, and probably the least likely person of that particular hour to be able to make a sound decision on the matter, even though I was by that time completely sober.

"What if I fire you, Mr. Lincoln, as my counsel on this matter, and defend us myself?" I suggested as my alternate plan.

"That's the best idea you've had yet," he announced gleefully, tipping his hat, and turning to walk away.

"Wait, Mr. Lincoln," I pleaded. He stopped and turned back towards me. I hung my head, and told him emphatically, "I think I'll just plead guilty and take my chances."

"Great idea, Hill," Mr. Lincoln shouted. "Why didn't I think of that?"

We both pleaded guilty. Kilpatrick and I were each fined one dollar. Nothing more was said about the matter.

But I think Mr. Lincoln liked the fact that I stood my ground, fought with all the resolve I could muster to defend my indefensible position, and then admitted I was wrong. He seemed to admire those traits in me, while at the same time thinking I was foolish in my actions.

He also reminded me of the lesson about talking my way out of the situation instead of using my fists. "Have you forgotten what we talked about? You said you would think on it."

"No sir, I haven't forgotten. Instead of thinking about it, it is time to act on it," I suggested.

I saw our friendship develop into a closer bond from that day forth.

That case is another example of how Mr. Lincoln operated. He was a strong proponent of compromise as a first choice, with a trial being his last choice. Many a time, as in my case, he sat the parties down and tried to resolve the dilemma without going into the courtroom. He helped people settle their conflicts satisfactorily prior to trial and at the same time, removed those cases from the full docket that faced us each day in Judge Davis' courtroom.

Chapter 6

After some time riding the circuit with Mr. Lincoln, I was invited to a gathering at his home in Springfield. I was excited to have been put on the guest list.

Dressed in my fanciest green velour suit with plaid vest and a ruffled shirt, I carried my tall hat and my fancy cane. Upon entering their home, Mr. Lincoln introduced me to his wife, Mary. Right away, I found myself intrigued by the lady he had told me just a little bit about. I was picturing in my mind the scene of Mr. Lincoln trying to tiptoe around this house, and I couldn't help but smile.

I had heard from other lawyers that Mrs. Lincoln was a screaming maniac, sometimes even ranting and raving at her husband in public. Whenever anyone talked about her, they described her as either insane or a demon. I had heard that she was fiery and argumentative with most anyone. Actually, I admit, at the time I was not looking forward to meeting her.

Surprisingly, I found Mrs. Lincoln quite pleasant. She was eloquently dressed in a bright blue dress with a broad hoop skirt. Buttons adored the front, from her neck to her waist. I wouldn't call her pretty, but I would say that she certainly carried herself with dignity and grace. She didn't appear overly happy and content, but she didn't seem to be a demon or a screaming maniac either. But perhaps I would have to be with her more times to be sure.

Mrs. Lincoln was at least a foot shorter than her husband, if not more, and was as portly as he was skinny. Side by side, they were definitely a mismatch.

Before I had a chance to offer any intelligent comments, Mr. Lincoln excused himself and went off to greet another guest. That left me alone with Mrs. Lincoln. I was uncomfortable with the thought that I had been abandoned by my friend to carry on alone with his wife.

We were offered drinks by a colored servant and I

grabbed one for courage. He took my hat and cane. Mrs. Lincoln led me into the library and invited me to sit with her.

"Mr. Lamon, may I call you Hill?" she asked.

I nodded my approval. "Certainly, Mrs. Lincoln," I answered, "that's what your husband calls me."

"Please call me Mary," she insisted.

"Mrs. Lincoln, not being disrespectful, but my mother taught me that I should never call an adult by her first name," I admitted sheepishly. "Your husband is always Mr. Lincoln to me."

"You may call me Mrs. Lincoln, but it makes me sound older than I am," she joked. "Are you enjoying your time on the Eighth Judicial Circuit?"

"I am learning more than I could have imagined," I admitted. "Being fresh out of school, I had the impression that I was ready to walk into the courtroom and face the jury in any situation from misdemeanor to murder. I have certainly found out how wrong I was."

"Do you enjoy being on the road so often?" she asked.

"Actually I like being in a different courtroom from week to week," I told her. "Each county seat is a new experience for me."

"I could love Abraham more if he were home on a more regular basis. The boys and I miss him. I think the terms of the circuit keep him away too long."

"My wife Angeline would agree with you. She complains that I am always gone."

"Are you and your family enjoying Danville?" she inquired.

"Yes, ma'am. It is a charming little community, though much different than what I was accustomed to in Virginia."

"In what way?" she asked.

"It's kind of hard for me to explain, ma'am. People here are just different – not in a bad way. In Virginia, there was a gentry on the upper level and then the rest underneath. Here I don't see those distinct layers."

I was enjoying my conversation with Mrs. Lincoln. After a few minutes of being in her presence and bantering back and forth with trivial conversation, it was apparent that she was quite bright and refined. Her demeanor put me at ease. The rumors I had heard, that she was "a devil in a dress" or that Mr. Lincoln stayed away "to keep the peace in the house" seemed to have been exaggerated. Perhaps she was just on her good behavior for the evening. I was certainly attempting to behave myself while in her company. In fact, I turned down an offer of another drink after I had drained the first one.

I found Mrs. Lincoln bright and lively, and quite easy to talk to. She was flirting with me a bit, I think, though I certainly didn't mind. She was better educated than most women I knew. Smart women are an attraction to me.

I looked around to see if Mr. Lincoln would be coming back, but it didn't look like that was going to happen soon. I remained on my own, trying to live up to my admission that I was comfortable around women.

"Abraham is quite fond of you, Hill" she added cheerfully. "He talks about you often. You are always mentioned in his letters to me. He thinks you are very smart and a promising new lawyer. I know he enjoys your company and counts you as his friend. I hear that you make him laugh. He appreciates that. And he loves it when you play your banjo and sing."

"I enjoy being with your husband wherever we go, Mrs. Lincoln. You would not believe how people flock to the courtroom when he is defending a client," I told her. "He is certainly a crowd favorite all along the circuit. Mr. Lincoln is always quick witted and jokes frequently. I have learned so much from him about how the courts work. And I appreciate the other lessons that he has taught me."

Mrs. Lincoln pulled me closer and said she would share a secret with me if I promised not to tell. I promised.

She whispered in my ear, "Mr. Lincoln is a great favorite everywhere. He is to be president of the United States some day. If I had not thought so I never would have married him, for you see, he is not pretty. But look at him. Doesn't he look as if he would make a magnificent president?"

I turned toward Mr. Lincoln. She certainly was right about one thing. No one could ever call Mr. Lincoln "pretty." But the thought of him as president of the United States was a rather outrageous idea for me. In fact, at the time, in spite of my admiration for him, I did not find him a promising candidate for the presidency.

I stammered in responding, hoping Mrs. Lincoln didn't notice. "Certainly, Mrs. Lincoln, he would make a fine president."

She just nodded. In my head, I was trying to figure out just where her suggestion had come from.

Finally Mr. Lincoln came by and said he needed to introduce me to others at the gathering. I excused myself from his wife, and we walked toward a distinguished looking couple on the other side of the room.

After an enjoyable evening, Mrs. Lincoln insisted that I return to their house sometime soon. I agreed to do that. A colored servant retrieved my hat and cane. And I left to ride to my home in Danville.

Over the time that followed I thought about Mrs. Lincoln's "secret" often. Each time I just shook my head. It was about the most outlandish prediction I had ever heard in my life. I did not think the Mr. Lincoln that I knew was going to be president some day.

Chapter 7

In 1852, information I gathered for Mr. Lincoln helped him win several important court cases.

During a conversation at the Vermilion County courthouse that we were having about the proceedings of court, he brought up a subject I had not expected.

"Hill," Mr. Lincoln said, motioning me to come closer as if he had something important to discuss. "It has occurred to me that you are the brightest new lawyer around."

I was surprised by the praise, especially coming from him, but as my usually brazen self, I answered smartly, "I am pleased that you noticed, sir. I work hard at least in trying to give that impression," I offered, laughing out loud, amused by my own answer.

"Be serious, just this once, Hill," he insisted. "I am trying to engage you in an important matter. I am seeking a law partner. I feel that you are the person best suited to be that partner. How would you feel about my drawing up a contract for you to look at tomorrow?"

"I am quite surprised by your generous offer, Mr. Lincoln," I stammered, as by now I was certainly paying better attention. "I can't think of anyone who I would rather be partner with than you. I would be delighted to look over an agreement, though I am certain whatever you draw up, sir, would be fine with me."

I was elated, but a little confused. It occurred to me how helpful it would be for me to have a law partner with the reputation and experience of Mr. Lincoln. However, I could not quite figure out what advantage it gave him to partner with me, of all people. But that is what he wanted. And who was I to turn him down? I was surprised too because the offer came from out of nowhere.

I warned Mr. Lincoln that I may not be a "model" partner. "If I fall back into my old bad habits, it might bring embarrassment to you and our law firm, sir."

Mr. Lincoln, as usual, just laughed. "I see some values in you that you don't even see in yourself, Hill," he suggested. I waited for him to tell me what those were, but he didn't give me a list.

When I got home I couldn't wait to tell Angeline of my good fortune. "You'll never guess what happened today," I shouted before even removing my hat.

"Mr. Lincoln won that case with the railroad that you assisted him with, and you predicted that he was going to lose," she guessed.

"Yes, in fact he did win that case, but that's not the news I have. Mr. Lincoln has asked me to be his law partner," I proudly announced.

"Oh my God, Hill. I hope you accepted," she screamed, trying to wrap her arms around my massive body.

"I didn't hesitate for even one second. I was too afraid he would change his mind," I explained elatedly. "We will open a law office here and one in Springfield. I will bring in clients from this end of the circuit. And we should have a bit more money."

"Perhaps then I can start having some of the things I had grown accustomed to back home in Virginia," she was quick to point out.

Angeline had tolerated our meager existence but was never really comfortable or happy about it. I was not providing anything close to the life she had expected. And she let me know regularly how difficult that was for her to accept.

With our daughter, Julia Hill Lamon, being less than a year old, Angeline complained that under our present financial situation, it was difficult for the five of us to live.

I reminded her that better days were ahead of us. I secretly hoped that was true.

Mr. Lincoln's name on our sign certainly added great prestige to our practice. I got congratulated often on the streets when the locals found out about the partnership. Dr. Theodore was quite impressed, saying that of all the attorneys on the circuit, I could not have chosen a better partner. I guess Dr.

Theodore thought I chose Mr. Lincoln. I did nothing to relieve him of that impression.

The way the agreement between us had been set up, part of my job was to advertise and solicit new business, while Mr. Lincoln would meet with the clients and argue the cases. I would have clients scheduled to meet with us when we arrived at each courthouse for that particular week's trials. I thought that arrangement would work well for us.

Within the first few days of our partnership, Mr. Lincoln asked me how I became an attorney.

"I came to Danville, Illinois in the fall of 1847 to become a doctor, studying under my cousin, Theodore, I explained. "Before I got too involved with my studies, it became apparent that there was already an abundance of doctors in Danville. As I looked around the area, I decided a new doctor's pickings would be mighty slim."

"Theodore's brother, Bruce, had mentioned that lawyers were less abundant. He said there was a growing need for lawyers, especially since Danville was the county seat. I decided to study law instead. I read law under the tutelage of O.L. Davis, working long and hard. Mr. Davis encouraged me to pursue more formal training. He offered to lend me the money I needed to enroll in law courses at the University of Louisville, in Kentucky."

"I remained at the university and received a certificate to practice law in the Commonwealth of Kentucky. Soon after that, I applied for and received my license to practice in Illinois."

The only thing my new law partner said after I explained the scenario was "Dr. Hill Lamon doesn't fit you," and then he let the matter drop. I had to agree with that assessment.

Mr. Lincoln made his policy about accepting clients clear to me right up front. "If our client is not totally forthright in telling us the truth about their case, we will not defend him. It's as simple as that." I shook my head in agreement.

In the early days of the partnership, I learned from Mr. Lincoln what it meant to have impeccable integrity as I observed his dealings in even the most trifle matters. "You can't just be honest in the big matters if you aren't also honest in the small matters," he told me. "You are either honest or you ain't."

That negated my idea that I was "basically honest" in most instances. That was probably why no one called me "honest Hill" and why folks around here called him "honest Abe."

Before each court case, Mr. Lincoln and I sat down to discuss the direction of our defense for each client. "Here's the charges," he would explain with each new case. "What do you think is the best course of action for our defense?"

Whenever he asked my opinion, he expected me to know all the possible scenarios we might follow on our client's behalf. I appreciated that and learned from each situation. But it dawned on me later that even the times I disagreed with his direction, he never let it deter him from going down the opposite road. I figured out that just because he asked for my suggestions, it didn't necessarily change his mind or influence what he would pursue in the courtroom.

The highest percentage of our trials were civil cases, including many situations where someone sued to collect a debt, breach of contract, slander suits, land squabbles with the Great Western Railroad, adultery, bigamy, divorce, and others. We also occasionally defended clients in criminal proceedings including persons who stole cattle and horses, counterfeiters, and persons charged with assault and battery, trespass, larceny, keeping a disorderly house, murder and manslaughter. Our business was brisk. There were days when we represented at least one client for every case on the docket for that day.

In several civil cases, I was the defendant, one time being charged with trespassing and several times for not paying what someone insisted I owed. Mr. Lincoln was my attorney. I complained to him after the one case that I lost.

"Mr. Lincoln," I insisted, "I had the best attorney in Illinois defending me. How in the world did I lose the case?"

"Perhaps, young man," he joked, "the judge thought you were actually guilty as charged." Though I didn't lie to Mr. Lincoln, my law partner and friend, in that particular case of trespass, I was indeed guilty as charged. He probably knew that, although he never asked. And I was fined for my transgressions.

Our best known, of the one hundred fourteen cases we defended as partners, involved Mr. Scott, whose mentally unbalanced sister had almost ten thousand dollars. Mr. Scott had been appointed her conservator.

When his sister got married, her new husband asked the court to remove Mr. Scott as the overseer. Mr. Scott met with us and asked us to preserve his status against her new husband's wishes. He feared his sister's husband would quickly steal the money and disappear.

A fee of two hundred fifty dollars was agreed upon for our services. With the case being settled inside of perhaps twenty minutes at most, in Mr. Scott's favor, he was a very happy man. He approached me and handed me the money.

When I presented the money to Mr. Lincoln to put in the bank, he scolded me. "It is all wrong. The service was not worth that sum. Give him back at least half of it."

"But sir," I argued. "Mr. Scott agreed with the amount in advance of the case. He is perfectly satisfied with paying that fee."

"That may be," Mr. Lincoln insisted with a look of displeasure, "but I am not satisfied. This is positively wrong. Go, call him back and return half the money at least, or I will not receive one cent of it for my share."

I went and found Mr. Scott, returning half of his money. Mr. Scott was quite surprised.

That was the first, but not the last time, that Mr. Lincoln and I clashed on the amount to charge our clients. If Mr. Lincoln had his way on setting fees for services, we would have starved to death.

Mr. Lincoln took me aside after that case to make sure I got the lesson, and it wasn't about the money.

"Hill," Mr. Lincoln told me. "It doesn't matter that we got Mr. Scott a favorable verdict and that he was satisfied with the financial arrangements of the case. We cannot accept two hundred fifty dollars for twenty minutes of work — regardless of who the client is. Besides, that money comes out of the pocket of a demented girl. I would rather starve than swindle her. I never want the reputation enjoyed by those shining lights of the profession 'Catch 'em and Cheat 'em'. The lesson is about fairness."

"If you are right, Hill," he told me more than once, "don't ever relinquish your principle. Even if you are outnumbered 1000 to 1, if you are right, do not give up."

The other attorneys on the circuit were as troubled as I was when they heard about Mr. Lincoln's fees for services. "Lincoln, I have been watching you and Lamon," one lawyer insisted. "You are impoverishing this bar by your picayune fees. The other lawyers have reason to complain to you. You are almost as poor as Lazarus. If you don't make people pay you more for your services, you will die as poor as Job's turkey."

They informally charged Mr. Lincoln with "robbing his fellow attorneys by asking fees that were too low." In fact, they held a mock trial which became known as the "Ogmathorial Court" and found him guilty as charged in their kangaroo court. They fined him the cost of a pitcher of whiskey – which we then consumed as he watched.

Mr. Lincoln and I maintained two offices during our partnership. His office was in Springfield. My office was in the Barnum Building in downtown Danville, on the second floor above the tavern.

Several people asked me about the large ring-shaped stain that was very apparent on the top of my big office desk, claiming that ring was from the whiskey pitcher that was always present on my desk. I would say "always" is a pretty strong word for what really happened.

Our partnership lasted four years. It was dissolved by mutual consent when I was elected as the prosecuting attorney for the Eighth Circuit in the election of 1856. Mr. Lincoln had recommended I run for election for that position.

I continued to ride the Eighth Circuit but I was prosecuting cases rather than defending them. Often I tried cases against Mr. Lincoln.

In one instance, I remember quite vividly, I insisted in prosecuting a case when he had urged me to accept a plea. I should have listened to him, as his advice was usually very sound. I prosecuted anyway. The jury found his client innocent. He never said "I told you so" but on similar occasions, when it was a choice between a trial or a plea bargain, I accepted his judgment.

The majority of days, I would have chosen to prosecute against any other attorney in the world. But no matter the outcome of those cases between the two of us, we always ended up in the evenings discussing something of value.

When I became a lawyer, my goal was to become the best one on the circuit. But because of all the troubles I caused myself in trying to learn the complicated nature of the legal system, and because of troubles at home, I had fallen back on some familiar bad habits. One of the circuit lawyers wrote to his wife about his associates. "There are the usual lawyers in Danville. They are all well and behave themselves with remarkable decorum. Hill holds out." Can you imagine that? But he was right; my behavior was slipping.

Deep down inside I could have used my attorney skills to defend my behavior. Our daughter, Julia, had died before her second birthday. Both Angeline and I were devastated. I wandered aimlessly around the house, unable to do most anything at all.

Angeline had shut down and insisted that Julia's death was all her fault. Guilt hung on my shoulders like an old shawl. I felt guilty because I was on the circuit and wasn't able to come home before she died. And I added to my guilt because I didn't know how to comfort Angeline through those days following the funeral.

It seemed whenever anything important happened at home, I was on the circuit. And whenever I was home in Danville, I was either at work or at the tavern. Angeline pointed this out many, many times. For whatever reason, I chose not to correct that situation.

Admittedly, my drinking had become a problem again. And with the drinking came swearing and fighting. The three were always closely aligned in my life. I didn't beat up any more bartenders, but on one occasion I took a challenge to "step outside" only to find out that the man who was pushing me around inside the bar had reinforcements that came to his aid outside in the alley. I never hit the deck, and I dropped a few with my fists, but the outcome of their attack on my face was not pretty. Angeline barely recognized me after I stumbled home, bruise and bleeding.

It was Mr. Lincoln who spoke to me about it before it went any further. News traveled fast, and by the afternoon of the next day he had already sought me out.

"What's the other guy look like, Hill?" he asked. "You look a fright." I started to answer, but he stopped me dead.

"Hill," he said. "Everything you try, you are good at. You are even the best of anyone I know at being mischievous. Your destructive practices and your position as a practicing attorney don't mix. Remember me telling you that when I was growing up, I settled matters with my fists. It doesn't serve me any more. It doesn't prove anything."

He wasn't finished with me. "Your drinking and swearing and trying to pick fights doesn't serve you. I know you are feeling grief over your daughter's death. All of us can certainly understand that. But it's time you grew up. Even as successful a lawyer that I am, I sure wouldn't want to have to argue for getting you out of jail."

I was embarrassed. But I knew he was right. No one else would have said anything. Only my friend, Mr. Lincoln, cared enough to confront me about it.

"Sir," I offered dejectedly. "I have not known you to waste words, even on me. You are right. Although I am particularly good at causing trouble, I need to set those habits aside and concentrate on being a good lawyer and a good husband. Thank you for calling it to my attention."

"We probably will never have to discuss it again, my friend," he wisely added.

I hoped that he was right.

As good of an attorney as I was becoming, I continued to have troubles at home. Angeline was pregnant a third time.

But with my wife due to deliver in just a few of weeks, our second daughter, Kate Lincoln Lamon, who was less than a year old, was gravely ill.

"Hill, I cannot bare to see Kate sickly like this. It reminds me too much of what Julia went through," Angeline cried. She begged me to stay with her every minute of every day. I was not able to do that, but did provide neighbors and my sister Anna and her husband, William (who had recently moved to Danville) to help her.

I tried and tried to comfort her, but I didn't know how. She wouldn't let me close. I brought in Dr. Theodore Lemon, my cousin, to assure her that Julia's death was not her fault. He told her many babies in the area were dying and that the doctors had no medicine to prevent it from happening. She did not take kindly to his theory.

When Kate died on September 4, Angeline could not be consoled. Our friends feared her grief would cause the child inside her to die before birth. Once again, I was not much good in lifting her spirits. I held her hand for hours, but didn't know what to say to her. Each day she got weaker. It seemed like all her energy was seeping out through holes in her skin.

Just a little over two months later, on November 13, 1858, our third daughter was born. We were caught between the excitement of her birth and the fear that this child would not live long either. Because of the deaths of Julia and Kate, we were afraid naming her right away might be bad luck. I wanted to let her pick her own name when she got older.

Actually her birth was the least of my concerns. Angeline struggled through the process of childbirth and was ill for several months. My attention was split. I was trying to be attentive to my job on the circuit, to get help for Angeline to take care of a new baby while she was ill, and to support her as a caring husband. Fortunately I would be home until the circuit convened again in March.

As time went on, Angeline seemed to lose her will to live. She woke me up almost every night, screaming as her dreams were frightening her. A fever attached itself to her and would not go away. She cried constantly, fearing our third child would die too. Angeline continued to tell anyone who would listen, that the deaths of our two daughters were totally her fault. The birth of our newest baby girl had been too much strain on her. She was almost insane with grief already. I tried desperately, but was helpless to say anything that she found comforting. I might as well have not been there at all.

Finally, she lost her battle totally and died, just five months after our daughter was born.

My colleagues on the circuit, following the lead of Judge Davis who postponed court for several days, all came to her funeral. I was grateful for that. I had to be dragged from the cemetery by three men, as I had collapsed from the strain.

Mr. Lincoln and I discussed the tragedy of the deaths several times in the months following the funeral.

"I am quite angry at God for taking my two daughters and my wife away like this," I explained while wiping the tears from my eyes. I whined further. "I couldn't be in two places at once. I wasn't good when I was at home, and I was worse when I was on the circuit."

"Hill, I know what you mean," Mr. Lincoln offered in a consoling manner, placing his hand on my shoulder for a bit of comfort. "I don't believe in God in the Christian sense, but I grasp things that are in logical order in life. These three deaths certainly have no reasonable explanation. I wish I could explain why this has happened to you, but I cannot begin to understand myself. Know that Mary and I offer our deepest condolences and will help in any way we can. You just have to ask."

I appreciated his words of comfort.

Another time we talked, he brought up a similar loss in his life, one that I had forgotten about.

"I lost the love of my life at a young age too," he reminded me. "I never got over Anne Rutledge's death. I kind of understand what you are going through."

"I appreciate your thoughts on the matter, sir," I responded. "I am feeling pretty badly that I was never who Angeline wanted me to be. I was never home. She probably thought she made a mistake marrying me in the first place.

Her family never liked me. Did I tell you that before? I wanted to be a good husband, but my attention was always on something else. I was trying to be the best new lawyer on the circuit. I should have tried to be the best husband in Danville instead."

"I have had the same situation, Hill," my friend admitted. "Mary complains often that I spend much more time with you than I do with her and the boys. What is going to happen to your little girl?"

"My sister, Anna, offered to take her in. With all the time I was following the trials from one courthouse to the other, I certainly need her help. Topsey moved in with Anna to help her with the baby. I will spend all my time in Danville at Anna's house with my daughter. I owe Anna and the baby that."

After several months, that didn't seem to be working out either. My little girl, who Anna called Ann Morgan Lamon, looked so much like a little doll, that everyone started calling her Dolly. The name stuck. Dolly looked at me as if I were a stranger when I returned after being absent while on the circuit. Even though she seemed to be a happy child, she didn't act like she knew that I was her father. I watched sadly as she went to my brother-in-law, William, and wrapped herself safely in his arms whenever I got close.

It occurred to me that even though she was alive and healthy, I had already lost Dolly too.

Announcement of law partnership
From *Danville Citizen* newspaper 1852

Chapter 8

In May of 1860, Judge Davis took leave from the circuit and organized a group from Illinois to develop a plan for the approaching Republican National Convention at the Wigwam in Chicago.

Since I worked with Judge Davis, I approached him about letting me be a part of their efforts. He knew of my capabilities, had been impressed that I had learned quickly and had watched me become a successful attorney.

"Hill," Judge Davis admitted, "I hadn't thought about taking you to Chicago. Now that you mention it, I think I might be able to use your help. Please join us."

I was as excited as a schoolboy to be going to the convention. Although I had absolutely no political experience except in being elected prosecuting attorney, I looked forward to this as an important event for me. I was determined to do something to make a difference at the convention.

Our team's challenge was to see what it would take to nominate Abraham Lincoln for president. The Republican party of Illinois had instructed us to use all "honorable" means necessary to secure his nomination.

By this time, Mr. Lincoln had gained national exposure from the Lincoln-Douglas debates, held throughout Illinois and covered nationally by the newspapers. His Cooper Union talk in New York had brought major support outside of Illinois.

I knew where Mr. Lincoln stood on the issues. Usually he asked me to read the speeches before he gave them. Sometimes he even changed a word here or there upon my suggestion. I had attended several of the debates and was impressed by his presentations.

Most delegates coming to the national convention were committed to a particular candidate. None were committed to

Mr. Lincoln. Based on that, our goal was to encourage all the delegates to consider Mr. Lincoln as their second choice, if their candidate didn't get much support on the first ballot.

We had a formidable hurdle to overcome. William Seward, of New York, the heavy favorite for the nomination, had brought seventy delegates and thirteen railroad cars full of his supporters to Chicago.

The New York delegation by itself consisted of one-third of the votes Mr. Seward needed for nomination. And although we didn't know it at the time, they were prepared to offer Mr. Lincoln the slot on the national Republican ticket as vice-president if there was a second ballot. That move would have certainly put Mr. Seward over the top to win the nomination.

In our deliberations, we came to an agreement that we all needed to be very careful to neither disparage anyone's first choice nor to antagonize any of the delegates. And we were definitely told not to promise any political favors in the process. In fact, in Mr. Lincoln's telegram to Judge Davis, he instructed emphatically that "I authorize no bargains and will be bound by none."

Judge Davis, a savvy political veteran, coordinated all the canvassing. I was initially assigned to entertain the guests, to be a backup in case of any emergencies or to run errands.

Alcohol flowed freely at our headquarters. As I was determined from the outset to make a bigger impression on the outcome of the convention than the duties assigned to me, I abstained from drinking. At the same time, I was willing and eager to tell anyone who listened about our candidate from Illinois.

When our committee canvassing was done, Judge Davis broke down each state and assigned one of our men to contact all of their delegates individually. He let each man talk to those delegates he knew best. I was assigned to talk to the representatives from my native Commonwealth of Virginia.

Our team of Lincoln supporters worked behind the

scenes at all the hotels as delegates arrived for the convention. With not a minute to spare, we worked without sleep through the night to talk to as many delegates as possible.

While the committees argued the platform planks during the day, we continued working to try to reach every delegate we could find. Our plan worked well. We got assurances from many delegates that after the first ballot, they would abandon their favorite sons and vote for Mr. Lincoln. All we could hope for was that there would actually be a second ballot.

When the Republican platform was finally accepted, the Seward delegates urged Chairman Ashmum to start the balloting for the presidential nomination that same afternoon. Chairman Ashmum explained the ballots were not ready, and balloting would begin the following morning. That certainly helped our cause, as it gave us another night to try to convince the delegates to support Mr. Lincoln.

That evening and just hours before the actual voting was to start, Jesse Fell and I secretly met with Alexander Conner, without Judge Davis' knowledge. Mr. Conner, a newsman and lawyer from Indiana, knew where the tickets for the Wigwam had been printed. He took us to Mr. Hersey, the printer. Mr. Hersey agreed, for a substantial fee which we gladly paid in cash, to print extra delegate tickets and forget who asked him to print them.

The extra tickets printed were identical to the official delegates' passes. Mr. Conner, Henry Russel, Mr. Marshall and I worked through the night to list names of Lincoln supporters onto the tickets.

It was one of the most exciting and devious nights I had ever spent. If lightning would have struck the hotel that evening and I had been killed, there's no doubt in my mind that my soul would have completely bypassed the "pearly gates" and I would have had a free ticket straight to hell.

We knew that security regulations in the Wigwam allowed only delegates with official passes to enter the building. The tickets were checked each morning at the door by guards. With a limited number of seats, once the number of tickets for those admitted reached the building's capacity, no one else would be able to enter.

In the morning, our extra one hundred and eight Lincoln supporters took up seats where Seward's men were supposed to sit.

When Seward's supporters arrived in procession behind a marching band, one hundred and eight of his men carrying legal tickets were denied entrance. The Wigwam was already filled to capacity. Seward's men were furious, but their entrance into the convention hall was blocked by the guards.

Reports indicated that the sinister plot was actually my idea. At the time I didn't admit to it; but yes, the ticket printing idea came from my devious mind. It was one of my best ideas up to that time in my life. Surely it was a scheme with major implications. I was excited to have conceived the plan and to have actually pulled it off.

I had felt no need to tell the judge or anyone else in our group in advance what I was proposing; for fear that they would disapprove. I did not want the action squelched before it got off the ground.

Would Mr. Lincoln have approved of the extra tickets? No — never. "Honest Abe" would have been adamant that the vote that day should have been invalidated. He would certainly not approve of a "no good, rotten, cheating scoundrel" like me doing something that if it wasn't totally illegal, it was certainly border-line illegal. But remember, Mr. Lincoln was back in Springfield, and was not available for consultation. And, as he often did, even when he got suggestions from others on his ideas, he went ahead with what he thought needed to be done regardless of what anyone else said. He had taught me that lesson well.

Even with the successful ticket scam, there was still no guarantee that there would be any chance for Mr. Lincoln's nomination. We still had much work to do and needed an extraordinary amount of luck to be successful.

As the balloting began, Chairman Ashmum announced that a candidate needed to gather 233 votes to secure the

Republican nomination. We knew if any candidate received that number on the first ballot, those of us who supported Mr. Lincoln would go back home empty handed.

Of the men nominated, Mr. Seward was the clear favorite, but Salmon Chase and Edward Bates both believed strongly they would be nominated. Mr. Lincoln was definitely a long-shot.

When the votes were added up after the first ballot, no candidate gathered enough necessary for the nomination. At least one more ballot would be needed. We were ecstatic in our camp. Our plan was still alive and viable.

Mr. Seward finished first in the balloting with 173½ votes. Mr. Lincoln was a surprising second with 102 tallies. That was shocking to most of the delegates in the Wigwam.

Mr. Lincoln was clearly emerging as an alternative to Mr. Seward, which was what we had been suggesting.

The two most disappointed candidates were Mr. Chase and Mr. Bates. Mr. Chase finished fourth behind Simon Cameron of Pennsylvania. Mr. Chase had 49 votes to Cameron's 50½. Mr. Bates was just one vote behind Mr. Chase in fifth place.

The Chase and Bates' delegations would be under our watchful eye from that point forward, to see if their allegiance would shift with so little early support for their candidates. Our Illinois men, of course, were hoping the dislike and distrust that the Chase and Bates' delegates had for Mr. Seward would emerge as support for Mr. Lincoln. We were confident that individual delegates would break from the commitment they had on the first ballot. As Mr. Seward's support eroded, we were certain Mr. Lincoln's support would increase.

We thought the longer the balloting went on, the better chance our candidate had.

During the second ballot, there were even more surprises. First, Mr. Cameron withdrew his name from the voting. What we didn't know at the time was that Judge Davis had promised Mr. Cameron a Cabinet seat for dropping out of contention on the second round ballot and throwing

Pennsylvania's large block of votes to Mr. Lincoln.

Judge Davis had also secured Indiana's votes with the promise of the Secretary of the Interior position for Caleb Smith and the Secretary of Indian Affairs for William Doyle.

All three of those agreements were in complete violation of Mr. Lincoln's instructions. When questioned about his promises, the judge's attitude was "Mr. Lincoln is still in Springfield, and doesn't know what we have to go through. So we need to charge ahead and do whatever is necessary to win the nomination. And he will have to approve it."

The second ballot brought Mr. Lincoln enough additional votes to close the gap. Our candidate was now nearly dead even with Mr. Seward. The results showed Mr. Seward with 184½ votes, and Mr. Lincoln with 181. Mr. Chase and Mr. Bates received even fewer votes than on the first ballot, and were virtually eliminated from further competition.

As the third ballot proceeded, Massachusetts, Kentucky, Pennsylvania and Ohio threw additional votes to Mr. Lincoln, giving him a total of 231½ votes -- only 1½ votes from securing the nomination.

The loud and boisterous Wigwam crowd quieted in stunned silence when the totals were announced. I held my breath as Ohio's David Carter rose and asked to be recognized by the chair.

Mr. Carter spoke proudly, in a loud, booming voice, saying "I rise, Mr. Chairman, to announce the change of four of Ohio's votes from Mr. Chase to Mr. Lincoln." That gave our candidate the amount needed to go over the top. Abraham Lincoln was the Republican nominee for president of the United States.

There was pandemonium in the hall. The chairman pounded steadily on his gavel trying to call the convention to order. Delegates ignored the chair's request. The sound in the Wigwam was deafening. It took probably forty-five minutes to get the delegates to quiet down.

I, of course, couldn't restrain myself as I shouted, whooped and hollered until I was hoarse. I pounded my poor Lincoln team members on the back so hard many of them complained several days later that they had been beaten up during the victory party.

I wanted so badly to light a victory cigar, right there in the Wigwam, but thought better of the idea. I couldn't risk having the wooden structure catch fire with all those people inside. And I knew there would be time to smoke cigars and drink all night during the upcoming celebration.

The Seward supporters couldn't believe it. One I was close to looked like his best friend had just died. Mr. Seward's delegates who knew me as a Lincoln supporter stared daggers at me. If looks could kill, I would have been dead ten times over.

We had succeeded in grabbing the nomination away from the favorite Mr. Seward at the critical hour. And we had done it fair and square. Well, maybe that wasn't totally true. But in my mind, we had done nothing that Seward's supporters wouldn't have done in our shoes.

We couldn't wait to get the message to Mr. Lincoln in Springfield. I sent a telegram to him announcing the news.

We partied into the night, drinking and yelling like a bunch of school boys. I smoked about ten victory cigars and drank more than my fair share of whiskey. Not everyone from our team celebrated in a raucous manner. Several of the delegates from Illinois went instead to the nearby McVicker's Theater to watch the play "Our American Cousins."

We took the train back to Springfield the next morning. Judge Davis cornered me, urging me not to mention his promise of three Cabinet positions in direct defiance of Mr. Lincoln's instructions. He said if I agreed to that, he would not mention a rumor that he had heard concerning my involvement in the grand ticket printing scheme he was sure would not endear me to Mr. Lincoln. Without admitting to anything, we shook hands in agreement.

I was quite surprised when we arrived to find Springfield consumed with a carnival-like high-spirited party that lasted into the summer.

During the rest of the time before the election in

November, our team was focused to make sure Mr. Lincoln got as many votes as possible.

Our small group of dedicated supporters looked at poll books and wrote down the names of everyone who voted Whig in the last election. And we visited each person individually to encourage them to get out and vote for Mr. Lincoln.

Mr. Lincoln described his platform by saying "My politics are short and sweet, like a woman's dance. I am in favor of a national bank, the internal improvement system, and a high protective tariff. These are my sentiments and political principles. If elected, I shall be thankful; if not, it will be all the same."

He thanked me several times for my role in helping him garner the votes to win the nomination. He was very appreciative. But then he totally surprised me by saying, "What you did with the convention tickets, Hill, was totally despicable."

I was speechless. I did not have any idea how he might have found out. Before I could say anything he spoke again. "You still haven't decided to be completely honest, have you?"

"No sir, I haven't," I stammered. His comment had struck me right in the heart.

Now I was in a pickle. I had pledged to Judge Davis that I wouldn't say anything about the promises of Cabinet posts, but I needed to let Mr. Lincoln know. My secret had come back to haunt me.

On the eve of the election, Mr. Lincoln expressed concerned over what seemed to be an unraveling of the country. He feared President Buchanan might take some measures prior to leaving office that Mr. Lincoln would not be able to correct, if he were elected.

He pulled me aside and asked me to stay so we could talk. As usual, when he was troubled, he walked back and forth, practically wearing a path in the floor. He looked out into the night, as if I were not there. He was chewing on something important, and as he did at these times, he would mouth his thoughts to himself first. I knew he would talk to me when he was ready.

Finally he stopped pacing and spoke to me. "Hill," he said, looking quite frazzled, "as much as I am excited about the possibilities of becoming president, I have great reservations as to the enormous responsibilities the job brings with it. I just may have the most difficult task faced by a president since George Washington. I don't know if I am up to that."

I listened intently as Mr. Lincoln talked of the burdens that faced the country and the incoming president. "I have no political experience on matters as important as holding a whole country together," he confessed. "States are already threatening to secede from the Union if I am elected. Our nation is still young and may not be able to withstand having such a stern test as this."

"But no one else has any experience in these matters, sir. This is new. The nation has never faced this dilemma since it was formed," I suggested.

He nodded that he agreed. "I do not know where to turn, or who to turn to," he acknowledged. "Even the Republican candidates, who thought they would be nominated at the convention in Chicago, have distanced themselves from me. And I fear the final outcome of what happens to the Union will be used to judge me."

I assured him that I would be there to support him. I insisted that the others who helped would continue to do whatever he needed. "Perhaps Seward, Bates and Case will come forward in this crisis. The Republican platform is theirs too," I reminded him.

He pondered the situation and what I had said. At least on some level, I think he was mildly comforted by my assurances.

And then just before he walked out of the room, he offered me another of his great lessons. "We need to be very careful what we ask for."

Chapter 9

On Election Day, November 6, 1860, I woke early and voted for Mr. Lincoln in Danville. And then I rode to Springfield to be with Mr. Lincoln. Elmer Ellsworth, William Herndon, and I walked with him to the Sangamon County Courthouse around three in the afternoon where Mr. Lincoln would cast his vote.

A large crowd cheered Mr. Lincoln as we entered the building. He doffed his tall hat quite properly in recognition of their greeting (a new trick I had coached him on). When he came out with his marked ballot, he was quick to tell the three of us that he had voted for the state and local candidates, but had not voted for anyone for president. I asked him why.

"Hill, it would be quite unethical in this election to vote for myself," he replied. "If you want to be known as someone with integrity, you must stay above the situation in all matters."

"I don't agree on the voting, sir," I let him know. "What if you lose by one vote? If you don't think you are the best man for the job, how can you expect others to vote for you?"

"What's done is done, Hill," he answered smiling. "At least I didn't vote for any of the other candidates."

After he voted, we walked to Watson's Saloon to kill time before the election results would be arriving at the telegraph office. We already knew the outcome of elections in several states, as their voting had been completed earlier. The key vote for this day would come from New York with its large block of electoral votes.

There was still animosity from New York, since the convention failed to nominate their favorite son, William Seward. There was no certainty they would support Mr. Lincoln.

Several of the men went to the telegraph office to await

news of the national vote. They would send word to us.

Mr. Lincoln was troubled throughout the entire night. I thought whiskey could have calmed his nervousness. I made that suggestion to him, knowing full well he would not partake with us in the libation.

"Whiskey is not made to calm anything," he insisted. "Of all nights, this is not one I am about to give in to drinking. If I am elected, I want to have all my faculties about me to handle the victory. If I am defeated, I must surely be of sound mind and have a clear head to accept that as the will of the people."

We waited until around midnight. With each announcement that Mr. Lincoln won additional electoral votes, we toasted each other. Mr. Lincoln offered no response at all.

When the final results were in and it was announced that Mr. Lincoln had been elected president of the United States, guns were fired in the streets. Everyone in the saloon was excited and jubilant. They congratulated Mr. Lincoln, shaking his hand and slapping him on his back. He was the only person who didn't look excited by the news. The weary President-elect excused himself so he could walk home to tell his wife. The rest of us stayed to party some more. The celebration continued throughout the night and well into the early morning hours of the next day.

The election results were as follows:

Candidate	Popular Vote	Electoral Vote
Lincoln	1,857,610	180
Douglas	1,291,574	12
Breckinridge	850,082	72
Bell	646,124	30

Mr. Lincoln's electoral votes came from Maine, New Hampshire, Vermont, Massachusetts, Rhode Island, Connecticut, New York, Pennsylvania, Ohio, Indiana, Illinois, Michigan, Iowa, Wisconsin, Minnesota, California, Oregon and New Jersey. Fifteen states gave him no electoral votes at all. Mr. Lincoln and Vice President Hannibal Hamlin had not garnered even one popular vote in ten southern states.

It troubled us that although Mr. Lincoln won the electoral vote, he did not win the majority of the popular vote. In fact, Mr. Lincoln became the first president ever elected by a minority of the voters. As had happened in the Wigwam at the Republican National Convention, the split vote from a number of candidates had given Mr. Lincoln the victory.

Mr. Lincoln won the Illinois vote by more than 12,000 over his nearest opponent. He won Vermilion County (Danville) by 644 votes. But he came in second his home district, Sangamon County (Springfield), 42 votes behind the leader.

"The people who know me best, Hill, did not vote for me. What does that say about electing me to run a whole country?" Mr. Lincoln asked.

"We live in a country," I reminded him, "where the majority rules. That doesn't mean they are right or wrong — just that you got more electoral votes. Let's just hope, in this instance, those who know you best are mistaken." I did not remind him that the man who absolutely knew him best of all had not voted for himself for president.

With Mr. Lincoln's election, the South called their legislators together to vote on secession as they had threatened to do.

From that day forth, Mr. Lincoln's political team who had worked so hard to secure the nomination and to get him elected, got pushed aside. There a great gush of excitement and enthusiasm of people now wanting to make Mr. Lincoln's acquaintance. They filled his home on a daily basis, leaving him almost no time to rest and plan his administration in Washington.

The Democrats had filled the patronage jobs for many of the last thirty years. Now all those clerk, paymaster, postmaster, port collector, and other jobs were vacant. And anyone and everyone came looking for a political appointment.

Among the earliest to arrive, just as I had predicted, were Simon Cameron, Caleb Smith and William Doyle, the three men Judge Davis had promised Cabinet positions in exchange for their states' votes in Chicago. I had told Mr. Lincoln that I knew these three men expected to be part of his Cabinet.

"But that was strictly against my orders, Hill," Mr. Lincoln stated. There was anger present in his tone. "I made it very clear that I did not want to be beholden to anyone."

"I know sir. I am aware of that. I am just telling you what honestly happened."

Meanwhile, it was no surprise that Judge Davis was not around. While others asked where Judge Davis was, I knew. He was hiding because he didn't want to be there when Mr. Lincoln learned of his scheme.

Several days after the election, the Republican leadership still insisted there was no impending crisis. I was surprised they thought there were no grounds that required any adjustment to their thinking and there was nothing to be concerned about. But I knew Mr. Lincoln was fretting the situation.

Chapter 10

Shortly after the election, Mr. Lincoln related this story to Mrs. Lincoln and me.

"I was returning home in the early morning hours following the announcement that I had been elected president. I went into my bedroom exhausted and collapsed onto a sofa. Near the couch was a large bureau with a mirror on it. I stared into the reflective glass at my face and experienced what many would term a vision. I think it had some very prophetic message."

"The reflection staring back from the mirror showing my face appeared to have two distinct but separate images appearing only about three inches apart. They disappeared and then reappeared as I watched myself in the glass. The images were clearer when they returned. Upon further inspection, I think the further of the two was much paler, reminding me of the color of death. The two views of my face were lost again and I fell asleep. I went back to the reflective glass several times since, during the day or the night, and the images returned."

Mrs. Lincoln and I went with him several times to the bedroom to try to see the images he had experienced. Neither of us were able to see any double image in the mirror.

"I think," Mrs. Lincoln explained, "the first, truer image is Abraham's first term as president. He saw the image in the mirror as clear and strong. I believe the second, more distant and less distinct image, is that of his second term, which he will not survive."

Where she got that cockamamie notion I have no idea.

While not being able to see the images he had seen, I certainly knew that Mr. Lincoln believed they had been there. But I think he and Mrs. Lincoln gave them much more importance than I would have.

Mr. Lincoln laughed at the incident a few days later,

calling the images hallucinations or some kind of imperfection in the glass itself.

Mr. Lincoln and I discussed the images several times. He asked for my impression. I told him I didn't think the less distinct image was anything at all about a second term. "It was just an optical illusion, sir," I insisted. "I don't think this country has re-elected a president to a second term in about three decades. Perhaps we should just focus on the four years that await you in Washington, and not worry about this curious vision or a second term."

For once, he agreed that he should listen to a bit of advice from me. And then he wanted to change the subject.

"Hill, tell me about your little girl. What is happening with her?" he asked.

"To tell the truth, sir, I am having problems," I admitted. "She is entrenched in my sister's family to the point that I feel like an outsider when I visit. And because of that, instead of visiting more, I visit less. I have become a stranger to her."

"Stephen Logan, my former law partner, told me that you were courting his daughter. Is there any news on that front?" he asked.

"Sally Logan is a charming lady," I said. "We are quite enamored with each other."

"Any chance of your little girl getting a new mother as a result?" he continued.

"It has always been hard for me to hide anything from you, sir. Yes, that is something we have discussed. In fact, with Sally's inability to have children, she would very much like to have my little girl, Dolly, as her own."

Mr. Lincoln was all smiles. "I see it in your face, Hill, that you are happy with this new situation."

It was true. I enjoyed Sally Logan's company. We had been spending a great deal of time together and seemed very compatible.

Sally was concerned about my daughter, as much as I was. While insisting that my sister was doing a great job of rearing Dolly, Sally argued for returning Dolly home to live with us. She told me the longer that Dolly lived with Anna and William, the more likely it would be that she would not want to be with us. "We will bring her here and raise her in our house, my dear," she insisted. "That is where she belongs, with her father and me."

I had explained honestly to Sally the disappointments of my marriage to Angeline, and promised Sally that I would be more attentive than before. "I was never home. That was not fair to Angeline. And I was not attentive when I was home. I was more interested in being a great attorney than a great husband. I will do better this time. I promise."

Mr. Lincoln offered that both he and his wife, Mary, supported my marriage to Sally Logan. Being from Springfield, they were certainly familiar with both Sally and her family.

"You have matured over the years that I have known you, Hill. You have learned many lessons and changed many of your bad behaviors," Mr. Lincoln commented. "I think you are better prepared now than last time. And we think Sally will make a great mother for Dolly."

"I appreciate your support, sir," I admitted, suggesting further that "since you know me better than anyone, perhaps you should negotiate a marriage contract."

Mr. Lincoln laughed. He was right about several things. I was more mature. I had learned lots of lessons and changed several of my bad habits. My fighting and swearing had been mostly cured. I had kept my drinking to times when Mr. Lincoln wasn't around, so even though he thought I had curtailed my drinking, that behavior hadn't really changed much. As usual, I was being "basically honest" with him, but not totally honest. And I agreed that it was important that Sally and I could be parents to my daughter, Dolly.

I proposed to Sally shortly after that discussion.

Late in 1860, Sally Logan and I were married in Springfield, Illinois.

Unfortunately, almost from the first day, my marriage to Sally had some of the same troubling signs from my previous marriage. Sally found my attention focused on my position as an attorney more than on her, and she didn't like it one bit.

"I thought when we got married you would be spending time with me," she yelled on more than one occasion. "You are always gone. Even when you are in Danville, you spend more time at your office than you do at home."

She was right.

I took her to visit Dolly. We wanted Dolly to come live with us. We were surprised and shocked that Dolly wanted to remain with Anna and William.

"So much for having a child, as you promised," Sally screamed. "Your own daughter doesn't want to be with you. So I have you to myself -- when you are home."

I couldn't stand the tension between us, but I was hearing arguments I couldn't refute. Even as good of a lawyer as I was, I couldn't defend myself against her charges.

I turned to my friend, Mr. Lincoln, for advice.

"I know you are busy, sir, making arrangements to go to Washington," I told him. "But could I have a minute?"

"I will always have time for you, Hill. How can I be of help?" he asked with genuine interest.

"I am doing it again, sir. I am repeating the patterns of my first marriage already. My new wife feels like anything and everything comes between us. And I fear that Sally has a good argument. Already I am focusing on my work rather than my marriage. And my daughter has chosen to stay with Anna's family rather than moving in with us."

"Hill," he counseled. "I will listen and advise you, when I can and where I can. You know that. But you also know one of my weaknesses is in dealing with the ladies. You are very good at everything you try. I have pointed that out many times. So what do you suppose that means, my friend?"

"That I am not trying in this instance, sir?" I asked.

"You hit the nail on the head, Hill. Now what are you willing to do about it?" he wondered out loud.

"I will have to think on that, sir. But I know that you are right."

"In previous matters, Hill, when you said you would think on it, you thought about the problem but never did anything about it," he pointed out. "This instance requires actions that are different than what you have done previously."

I wondered if I could change my behavior.

Sally Logan—Mrs. Ward Hill Lamon

Chapter 11

Following Mr. Lincoln's election, friends met with me to discuss how my work for Mr. Lincoln's nomination might be rewarded with a political appointment.

Traditionally, they told me, the president fills consulate positions around the world with his friends. They said I would receive what they called a "fat favor." I was told whatever position I asked for, Mr. Lincoln would approve as a courtesy to me. I was surprised by these developments as I had no concern that I be rewarded for anything I had done at the convention or in helping get Mr. Lincoln elected.

At their insistence, I thought about it. I had always dreamed of taking a journey to Europe. Their consensus was that the best post available was the consulate in Paris, France. The pay, I was informed, would be a substantial increase from my current legal work.

Sally liked that idea, seeing possibilities for a higher social level as Mrs. Ward Hill Lamon. She had already suggested that my position as prosecuting attorney might be traded in for a partnership in her father's Springfield law firm. My current salary was certainly nothing to crow about.

Following our discussions at home, I agreed to allow my friends to petition Mr. Lincoln for the appointment in France.

Those same friends also arranged a fancy title for me – as the governor of Illinois approved my appointment as Colonel of Artillery in the Illinois militia. It was an honorary title, for sure, bestowed upon me to take to Paris or wherever the president assigned me. A Zouave uniform was prepared and fitted. From that day forth, many of my friends and colleagues called me "Colonel" Lamon.

Mr. Logan (my father-in-law) and others sent letters to Mr. Lincoln urging my prompt appointment to the consulate of Paris.

But Mr. Lincoln had other plans. He asked me to come to

Springfield, as he wanted to talk to me. Upon my arrival there, he told me: "Hill, on the eleventh I will go to Washington. I want you to go with me. Our friends have already asked me to send you as consul to Paris. You know I would cheerfully give you anything for which our friends may ask or which you may desire. It looks as if we might have a war. In that case, I want you with me. In fact, I must have you. So get yourself ready and come along. It will be handy to have you around. If there is to be a fight, I want you to help me to do my share of it, as you have done in times past. You must go, and go to stay."

Before I could answer this surprising offer, he continued. "You know, Hill, that I will have little support in Washington. I am trying to pull together my political opponents for my Cabinet. I think they will agree to aid me with this difficult task. Congress does not meet until the fall. The country is in crisis. And I will be accepting the job as president of the United States, perhaps the most important position anywhere, with no experience in handling even a small portion of the job. Please, Hill, tell me you will go and help me."

Of all the men around him in Illinois who he could take to Washington with him, Mr. Lincoln told me he chose just two of his secretaries, John Hay and John Nicolay and me. That was all.

My mind raced to consider the implications of this surprising new situation. At first I was angry and disappointed. Washington was certainly known as a second class city. Politicians were not well thought of, and the town itself was said by many to be a filthy, mud hole even on a good day. My image of Paris was that it was a grand old city of distinction. There was hardly any comparison. Paris to me was all that would be good. My impressions of Washington were the opposite.

But I was also surprised at Mr. Lincoln's insistence. And as usual, his logic was hard to counter. He certainly could rely on me whatever the situation. He was sure that support would continue if I were there too. I do not think there was anyone else who he so completely trusted. This time he didn't even bother asking me what I thought. I knew my ideas would not have swayed his decision anyway.

The request made me proud but it also humbled me. I did not know why some of his life-long friends were not asked to go with him to Washington. I did know Judge Davis had asked for a federal court appointment. But he was not in Mr. Lincoln's favor because of disregarding his instructions at the convention.

Finally I answered him. "Sir, I am honored and humbled by your request," I stammered, while chewing on an unlit cigar. "I will go to Washington with you. Whatever challenges you will face, I will see to it that you do not face them alone. Or at least if you face them alone, you will have one friendly and supportive soul in your corner."

He shook my hand enthusiastically, pumping it up and down as if I had brought him the news that everything would be all right with the country. I hoped somehow that by going to be with him to Washington I could make a difference.

"Hill, to be honest," he added, "I am not sure what job I will assign you in the nation's capital. But I am certain that I want you there with me. Thank you for accepting my offer."

By the time of Mr. Lincoln's personal request, Sally and the others had gotten me excited about living in Paris. So when I was asked to go to Washington, I was sure they would all be disappointed.

Instead of Paris, my wife and I would be moving to Washington in the District of Columbia. Since Sally had already packed our household goods, it didn't seem to me a change in plans would be all that disruptive, though I did realize that Paris was much more her style than Washington.

I was not sure what Sally's feelings would be on the change in plans. I hurried home to tell her of the new development, even though I had not consulted her before telling Mr. Lincoln of my decision. Sally was less than overjoyed. In fact, I have never seen anyone so disappointed in my entire life.

"Our new marriage up to this point has been one big

disappointment after another. Your promises of having your little girl live with us and of your being home with me have been empty," Sally exclaimed bitterly, throwing several pieces of fine china in my direction as she continued. "You excite me with tales of Paris, an increase in salary, and finally living in style. And now you are going to Washington. And you expect me to embrace the idea. I will not go. I prefer Illinois to Washington. There is nothing in Washington that I would have the slightest interest in."

In picking up the pieces of the broken china which fortunately had not hit me, I realized that all her complaints were true. I didn't think she would ever stop crying. And I was not sure she would ever move to Washington. "Suit yourself. Remember that Dolly doesn't even acknowledge me as her father. I want to be close to Dolly, but it seems the feeling is not mutual. I dreamed of going to Paris too. And now you tell me that there is nothing in Washington that you have the slightest interest in – which I am assuming means me."

I knew I had made the right decision. And I was not real sure if it mattered to me at that point whether Sally followed me there or not. Mr. Lincoln needed me to go with him. In essence, I realized I had chosen Mr. Lincoln over my own new wife.

Eventually my enthusiasm, more promises I wasn't sure I could keep, and my charm wore Sally down. She was even considering a new life in the nation's capital.

As for me, I would travel with Mr. Lincoln to Washington. Sally would join me there after I got settled in my new job. When and if that would ever happen would be decided at a later date.

Meanwhile, the Union Mr. Lincoln was inheriting was already starting to dwindle. South Carolina was the first to vote, deciding to secede on December 20.

From January 8 to January 18, Florida, Mississippi, Alabama and Georgia voted to support secession.

Even while this was all happening, Mr. Lincoln continued to hope for a restoration of the Union by peaceable means.

But the Republicans were changing their tune. They were now fearful of a disruption of the Electoral College vote, violence at the Inauguration, and an attack on the capital.

But all the news was not totally distressing. On February 4, the Commonwealth of Virginia (my home state) defeated a secession resolution 122 to 30. On February 9, Tennessee followed suit, allowing its citizens to vote and defeating the secession legislation 91,803 to 24,749. In Kentucky, a call to convention was defeated. And in Missouri, their convention voted 89 to 1 against secession.

Mr. Lincoln was encouraged by those votes. "Hill," he exclaimed joyously. "The tide is turning back. The Commonwealth of Virginia's vote in particular, is very important." I was pleased that my home state had voted against secession.

Chapter 12

The president-elect wanted to make a grand entrance into the nation's capital. He asked some of his staff and friends to plan an elaborate train adventure that would take him through the North to thank those citizens who had elected him.

Mr. Lincoln and his family were to travel through twelve northern states. The trip was scheduled to take twelve days, cover over 1900 miles, and would involve twenty-three separate railroads. The Lincoln train would proceed very slowly, to give anyone along the way the opportunity to come out and see their newly elected President. We would leave Springfield on February 11, 1861 and arrive in Washington on February 23.

I thought the train trip idea was a brilliant one. The people of the North needed to get to know Mr. Lincoln because certainly he would look to them for their support with a war looming on the horizon.

The newspapers were prepared to deliver reports of Mr. Lincoln's stops and speeches at the major cities. The reports would filter back to every community, even those the train didn't pass through. Persons who voted for Mr. Lincoln but didn't get to see him along the way could read about him and get to know him through the newspaper reports.

The trip was also important because almost simultaneously, the newly elected president of the Confederacy, Jefferson Davis, was traversing parts of the South by train. I knew the comparisons of the two trips would be fodder for the newspapers.

Our plan and schedule had been published in the newspapers prior to the Mr. Davis announcement of his train trip. It was obvious Mr. Davis was grandstanding and copying Mr. Lincoln's idea. I was angry that Mr. Davis was taking a train trip too. I passed the information on to Mr.

Lincoln, telling him I thought Mr. Davis needed to come up with an original idea.

"Hill, calm down," Mr. Lincoln insisted, giving me an enthusiastic scolding. "Whatever Mr. Davis is doing is of no consequence to us. It is important that we do not react to anything that he is attempting."

I was still fuming, but agreed to disagree. Without expressing it to Mr. Lincoln, I personally thought whatever Mr. Davis was doing was of prime concern for us. Even if no one else cared what he was doing, I was going to keep a wary eye on Mr. Davis.

The presidential party assigned to ride the train with Mr. Lincoln included his son, Robert, John Hay, John Nicolay, Dr. William S. Wallace (Mr. Lincoln's personal physician and also his brother-in-law), Norman Judd, Judge David Davis, Major David Hunter, John Pope, O. H. Browning, George Hazard, Illinois Governor Richard Yates, Captain Elmer Ellsworth of the Chicago Zouaves and myself.

Mrs. Lincoln and their other two sons, Tad and Willie, were scheduled to take another train and to meet us in Indianapolis.

The procedure at each of the small towns we passed through was to have Mr. Lincoln stand on the platform on the back of the train and wave as we slowly passed. Receptions would be held and speeches would be arranged in the major cities.

Since Mr. Lincoln was the first president ever elected west of the Appalachian Mountains and therefore most likely the first one many of these folks would see, excitement levels were quite high.

At every stop, bands were scheduled to play and parades were to be held. The goal in each city was for every political leader possible to be allowed to appear on the platform with Mr. Lincoln.

Like the towns themselves, the major railroads each wanted the Lincoln train to be pulled by their fanciest new locomotive. They insisted the president-elect had to ride in their best railcar. With railroads having various track gauges, often Mr. Lincoln would have to leave one train and board another. This resulted in a logistical nightmare. All the time, the train needed to be kept as close as possible to the nationally published schedule.

Mr. Wood of New York made all the preparations for the lengthy and very complicated trip. His massive publication called "Circular of Instructions" spelled out each and every detail.

Mr. Lincoln said he read Mr. Wood's report and agreed with the plan. I read it and was troubled with the plan as it scared me that so many people would have up close access to Mr. Lincoln at almost every point along the way. I voiced my concerns, not to Mr. Lincoln, but to Mr. Wood. Mr. Wood said he didn't need my approval, as he already had Mr. Lincoln's.

The train was scheduled to leave Springfield, Illinois at 8:00 a.m. on February 11. A large crowd of well wishers was waiting to say goodbye when the Lincoln party arrived at the Great Western Railway station at Tenth and Monroe Streets. Mr. Lincoln shook hands with as many of the folk present as he could, to be interrupted only by the arrival of the train.

Before we left the station, Mr. Lincoln appeared on the train's rear platform and spoke briefly to his friends. He bid them a fond farewell. It sounded to me like he was unsure if he would ever return.

The train pulled out of the station on time, heading toward Washington City. I shook Mr. Lincoln's hand, telling him I thought his short talk there had been quite appropriate and well received.

I was surprised, as I think Mr. Lincoln was, at the lines of people along the train route. People waved and yelled as the train passed. Mr. Lincoln returned to the rear platform of the train to wave to them. I stood next to him, not quite believing all the thousands and thousands of people we passed along the route.

"Hill," Mr. Lincoln said to me. "I am truly amazed how many people have come out to get just a glimpse of me. Do you suppose that there will be large crowds in the cities too?"

"Yes, sir," I responded. "I am quite sure there will be hordes of people at every town along the way wanting to catch a glimpse of the newly elected president."

The train made a short stop at my hometown of Danville. There hundreds of well wishers came out to greet us. I recognized many of my friends and neighbors as I watched Mr. Lincoln reach down from the train and shake hands with as many folks as he could reach. Several people shouted "Hill" and I waved to acknowledge their presence. I spotted my wife, Sally, in the crowd. She waved to me, but she looked sad. Her gesture lacked any enthusiasm whatsoever.

Colonel Edwin Sumner joined us at State Line, and told me that he had uncovered a plot to harm Mr. Lincoln when the train got closer to Washington. I suggested we could discuss that at length in a few days. I had no time to worry about a situation that was still a long way off.

We proceeded through Indiana and to Indianapolis where we were to stay overnight at the Bates Hotel. There Mr. Lincoln became very annoyed, in fact, angrier than I had ever seen him. He had entrusted his satchel to his oldest son, Robert. The bag contained Mr. Lincoln's only copy of the upcoming Inaugural speech.

When Mr. Lincoln asked Robert for the satchel, Robert didn't know where it was. Mr. Lincoln screamed at his son, lambasting him in front of a dozen dignitaries for his carelessness.

We began to search the hotel for the satchel. The president-elect had spent hours writing the document. It was currently only in draft form. If the speech were found and publicized in the newspaper prior to the Inauguration, there might be embarrassments.

We looked in the hotel baggage room, finding what we thought was the proper bag. Mr. Lincoln's key fit, but when I saw a bottle of whiskey inside, I knew immediately we had found the wrong bag. A little later I found Mr. Lincoln's satchel with the speech intact.

From that point, Mr. Lincoln took personal control of the

speech by removing it from the satchel and placing it inside his hat where he always kept his most important papers.

The incident with Robert left me quite surprised at Mr. Lincoln's anger. Personally I thought his outburst was way too harsh for the situation.

There was little doubt that Mr. Lincoln was under a lot of stress with the states in the South continuing to vote for secession, and the Union crumbling on a daily basis. In my experience, it has always been easier to lash out at someone close (like Robert) when the bulk of Mr. Lincoln's anger was certainly targeted to the South -- a much more distant foe.

I talked to him about the problem. "I scared myself," he admitted, "with my anger toward Robert."

"You scared me too, sir," I told him. "Anger doesn't serve you, but I think sometimes we need to get it out of our system."

"I appreciate, as always, your thoughts on the matter," he said. "I am usually the one telling you that you should curb your bad habits, Hill. I am embarrassed that you have had to suggest the same to me. I guess those darn southern states have me riled up to the boiling point, and Robert just got in the way."

"Yes, sir," I offered. "I believe that's exactly what happened."

It was at this point that Jesse Dubois and his cronies from Illinois imparted their threat upon me regarding what they would do to me if anything happened to Mr. Lincoln while he was in Washington.

Mr. Dubois and his friends didn't know me. I had messed up with Mollie Pultz. I had lost two daughters and my wife, Angeline. My daughter, Dolly, didn't even acknowledge that I was her father. I had perhaps already lost my new wife, Sally, as I wasn't sure she would ever move to Washington. I was not going to lose my best friend, Mr. Lincoln. He was all that I had left.

Later that same evening, I finally got a chance to sit with Colonel Sumner and let him air his concerns about Lincoln's safety as the train approached Washington.

"I have received information, confirmed by both my father and General Winfield Scott, of a plan to injure, kidnap or perhaps even kill Mr. Lincoln when the train reaches Baltimore," Colonel Sumner related. He told me the details of the information they had gathered.

And then he continued. "General Scott thought it important that you know the situation in order for you to take whatever precautions you think will be necessary. Please, I beg you, Lamon. Consider these threats very seriously. Be careful who you tell this information to, as there might be someone on the train who is working with those trying to harm him."

"I will take the matter under advisement and discuss it with Mr. Lincoln," I assured him. "I appreciate your concern. I realize that this highly publicized train trip will expose Mr. Lincoln to many situations that may be hazardous. I will do everything in my power to see that nothing happens to him."

If I had not taken my duties as Mr. Lincoln's bodyguard seriously to this point, I now had even more reason to be aware of the dangers the president-elect was facing.

On the morning of February 12 (Mr. Lincoln's fifty-second birthday) we departed, traveling toward Cincinnati. The Lincoln family (Mary, Willie and Tad had joined us in Indianapolis) rode the fourth car.

In Cincinnati, large crowds listened as Mr. Lincoln spoke again.

Every minute that I could, I was trying to be vigilant in making sure the train trip was safe. There was possible danger at almost every turn, with bridges to cross, remote areas of the countryside to traverse and huge crowds expected at all the major stops.

My two eyes alone could do very little to scout the area at every one of Mr. Lincoln's appearances, though I tried the best I could. I was virtually alone in my mission. I stood beside him each time he spoke or just waved from the platform at the rear of the train. I stayed by his side during each parade and speaking engagement in the larger cities.

Each local police organization had been asked to provide

men for the train's arrival, but in every instance their job was to keep roads cleared for Mr. Lincoln's entourage to pass through and not specifically to protect Mr. Lincoln. I worked overtime to try to examine the possibilities in every direction at once.

As weary as I was, I had to keep at least one eye open at all times. I swore off alcohol for the entire trip (a huge sacrifice for me) so I would not be impaired in the least. I slept only a few minutes here and there. As tired as I was, the assignment was energizing me.

The morning of February 13 (Wednesday) was a troublesome one as I read reports of that day's Electoral College vote in Washington, D.C. There were predictions that the vote would be disrupted. If the votes were not cast, no president would be elected. I also heard reports from newspaper men on the train of possible Southern plots to take over Washington.

General Scott reportedly had assured Mr. Lincoln he would post guards at the Capitol entrance and also at the doors leading to the House floor where the electoral voting would take place. He also promised to have the vice-president oversee the balloting.

We traveled to Columbus, where Mr. Lincoln addressed the Ohio Legislature. And then we were taken into Governor Dennison's office where Mr. Lincoln was handed a telegram from General Scott concerning the Electoral College vote we had worried about. The telegram read: "The votes were counted peaceably. You are elected." We cheered loudly. We congratulated Mr. Lincoln. He went to bed after telling me, "Now the work begins."

Following our stay in Columbus, we departed, moving slowly in an easterly direction through small towns in Ohio. We arrived in Pittsburg at the end of a very long day.

On Friday morning, February 15, the president-elect received cheers from the largest crowd of any we had seen up to this point. Mr. Lincoln gave a short speech. He had been bothered by a sore throat. I was afraid if he spoke at length his voice wouldn't last the remainder of the trip.

His speeches were troubling to me. His topic seemed to be that life was wonderful. I confronted him about his message. "I am concerned, sir, that you seem to be telling the people along the way that nothing is happening around the country – as if the Southern states weren't leaving the Union," I told him. I was trying to get him to see that he wasn't focusing on reality and was ignoring the huge problem looming on the horizon.

He responded quickly. "Trust me, Hill. I know what I am doing."

I did trust him. I just wasn't sure about that second part of his statement. I feared Mr. Lincoln was underestimating the crisis and compounding the situation by pretending it wasn't important.

It was interesting. Here I was, a man who was more interested in the limelight and a good story than the truth. Now I was suddenly concerned that "honest Abe" wasn't telling the whole truth to the very people who had trusted him to be their new president. For that moment, it was an intriguing switch of our positions.

My perception was that Mr. Lincoln thought the people of the South were too smart to ruin the government. I really think he was of the opinion that the country would save itself, and that conciliatory policy and gentleness could prevent secession. He trusted proper policy would save the Union. I was not convinced. But he was the president, and I was not.

Later I told him "I have information from informed sources, and brought to me by Colonel Sumner, that General Winfield Scott and Sumner's father think there is a plan to injure, kidnap or kill you when the train reaches Baltimore."

He listened intently and let me finish revealing the details Colonel Sumner had told me. And then he cut me off, saying "Hill, we will not have another word on this ridiculous matter." With that he walked back to the presidential car.

For me, the matter was a legitimate concern, not ridiculous at all. And a matter I would have to confront before passing through Baltimore. Though I didn't discuss the possible trouble again, I continued to worry about the information that had been relayed to me. At the time, I didn't have a plan, but I still had about a week to think about how we might avoid problems in Baltimore.

We boarded the train and journeyed onward to Cleveland, Ohio, where Mr. Lincoln spoke again to an extremely large and very enthusiastic crowd.

On Saturday, February 16, we left Cleveland and the train moved along toward Buffalo. We were greeted there by former President Millard Fillmore. Mr. Lincoln spoke at the American House.

On Sunday, February 17, the train sat silent as railroad representatives had argued it was not proper to continue the trip on the Lord's Day. Mr. and Mrs. Lincoln attended church and dinner with Mr. Fillmore.

I barely slept as I imagined everything that could go wrong. The publishing of the entire trip schedule (against my best advice) opened up the possibilities for organized groups to be waiting at every point. Strangers boarded the train at each stop to meet Mr. Lincoln. I had no boarding list, so I saw everyone as a possible threat.

Conspirators cutting the telegraph wires could easily commandeer the train and take Mr. Lincoln hostage. Or worse. I constantly tried different scenarios in my head, any one of which could have easily led to disaster. It was easy for me, having a background of causing mischief, to conjure up ways to disrupt the train or harm the new president. The worry caused me to have a headache for the whole trip.

On Monday, February 18, the train continued on to Rochester and then to Syracuse.

After a very short stop in Utica, we moved toward Schenectady. There Mr. Lincoln emerged from his rail car all decked out in a new broadcloth overcoat and hat provided by Mrs. Lincoln. I had to admit the new outfit improved his appearance quite noticeably.

A *New York Times* reporter noticed his new clothes and commented in his newspaper, "Since then Mr. Lincoln has looked fifty percent better. If Mrs. Lincoln's advice is always as near right as it was in this instance, the country may congratulate itself upon the fact that its president is a man who does not reject, even in important matters, the advice and counsel of his wife."

At Troy, Mr. Lincoln's message was brief, saying "The country need not be saved, for it 'will save itself', and that only the institution of the country needed protecting." So you see what I meant about his peculiar thoughts that the nation was not facing crisis and that everything would just work out. I was not convinced, although I certainly may have been in the minority.

In Albany, Mr. Lincoln spoke directly to the state legislature. While there we received a telegram informing us that Jefferson Davis had been inaugurated that same day in Montgomery, Alabama as the president of the Confederacy. Mr. Lincoln's friend, Alexander Stephens, was sworn in as the Vice-President.

"I am greatly disappointed, Hill, that my friend, Congressman Stephens, disavowed his allegiance to the nation he had loved so much," Mr. Lincoln told me.

Although Mr. Lincoln had obviously been aware that this would happen, I think the news raised the event from mere speculation to reality.

"Sir, perhaps it is better to have a known enemy next to Mr. Davis than someone you don't know," I suggested to him.

He shook his head in agreement.

On Tuesday morning (February 19) we left Albany to travel to New York City, arriving in mid-afternoon. We stayed overnight for two nights at the fine Astor Hotel.

In New York, the nation's largest city, crowds were estimated at about 200,000 people, more than I had ever seen at one place in my entire life. The possibilities here of harm to Mr. Lincoln were so numerous, I was totally out of my element as a one-man protection agency. Finally I was able to arrange for the Metropolitan Police chief to assign officers specifically for Mr. Lincoln's protection. I was grateful for that gesture.

On Thursday morning, February 21, we moved on to Philadelphia, arriving at 4:00 p.m. The presidential party stayed overnight at the Continental Hotel.

Pennsylvania Governor Curtin introduced himself to me in the hotel lobby. He evidently knew who I was, as he asked me to assure him that I was ready for any emergency that might arise on the trip. I opened my coat and showed him my own personal arsenal. It consist of two Colt 44 pistols, two Bowie knives, a black jack, brass knuckles and a hickory cane with a small sword hidden inside the handle. He left confident that I was ready for most anything.

Meeting the governor reminded me I had no plan for the situation presented by Colonel Sumner in Baltimore. I was not sure I could convince Mr. Lincoln to do anything differently than what the schedule called for anyway.

Mr. Lincoln was especially looking forward to the next day's itinerary. On February 22, he would be speaking at Independence Hall, a place he considered hallowed ground.

We were anticipating more huge crowds there.

Chapter 13

What we weren't anticipating in Philadelphia was news of more possible trouble. Samuel Felton, president of the Philadelphia, Wilmington and Baltimore Railroad, contacted me at the hotel and insisted on meeting with Mr. Lincoln at the earliest possible time.

I set up a meeting for that evening after all the receptions, speeches and hand shaking was finished. I had to practically drag a very weary Mr. Lincoln, Mr. Judd, Colonel Sumner and several others from the presidential party to the hotel room.

Mr. Felton quickly got the meeting underway. "We have confirmed reports about a possible attempt on Mr. Lincoln's life in Baltimore, uncovered by Allan Pinkerton and his agents," he explained. "I have brought Mr. Pinkerton with me and will ask him to give you more details. I know Mr. Pinkerton well enough to assure you that he will not in any case exaggerate." With that Mr. Felton introduced a stern looking well-dressed man of small stature who stood next to him. "This is Allan Pinkerton."

Mr. Pinkerton stepped forward and wasted no time in explaining the situation to those present.

"Gentlemen. I have sent my agents into Baltimore recently, as it is known as a hotbed of rebellious activity. Seven from my agency," he continued, "infiltrated a loose-knit band of radicals. My agents have uncovered an elaborate plot that involves a conspiracy between that fanatical bunch and the Baltimore police. The radicals plan to kill Mr. Lincoln when this train arrives in Baltimore."

He had certainly piqued our interest. We were all listening attentively as he continued. "The current arrangement calls for Mr. Lincoln's train to travel from Harrisburg to Baltimore on the Northern Central Railroad on February 23, with the train arriving at the Calvert Street

Station at noon. Mr. Lincoln is to be conveyed by open carriage through the streets, a distance of almost a mile and a half, to the Baltimore and Ohio Railroad's Camden Station for boarding the train to Washington."

"The plot my agents have uncovered," he explained, by that time speaking directly to Mr. Lincoln, "involves the police and Police Marshal, George Kane. Marshal Kane has agreed to send only a small detail to guard you, sir, when your train arrives. The radicals are planning a diversionary disturbance. All of Kane's policemen will investigate the disturbance, purposely leaving you totally unguarded. At that point, the radicals will attack you."

Mr. Pinkerton continued, wiping the perspiration from his brow with a handkerchief. "My agents report that the rebels are willing to give their lives, if necessary, to keep you, sir, from becoming president. Captain Fernandina, one of the lead conspirators, has boldly told my men 'Lincoln shall never, ever be president. My life is of no consequence. I am willing to give it for his. I will sell my life for that of the abolitionist.'"

"Another conspirator told my undercover agent, 'I will kill Lincoln before he reaches the Washington depot; not that I love Lincoln less, but my country more. I am ready to do the deed, and then I will proudly announce my name, and say 'gentlemen, arrest me, I am the man.' And then I will be called one that gave his country liberty.'"

"Conspirators," Mr. Pinkerton explained, "working with the Baltimore group, have been monitoring this train, and sending telegrams as to whether the train is on time at each stop. For the most part, the train is following the published schedule. The rebels are using ciphers to communicate without the telegraph operators knowing what they are doing."

Everyone in the room continued listening intently to the detective. I watched Mr. Lincoln's attention as it was riveted on the speaker. The whole time, Mr. Lincoln's expression did not change at all in spite of the implications of what he was hearing.

"The plot," the detective told us, "also involves a swift steam boat and crew, hired for the assassin and waiting in the nearby Chesapeake Bay, to facilitate the killer's escape. The boat will convey the killer to a southern port where he will be treated as a hero."

"In the final meeting, just last week," detective Pinkerton reported, "twenty conspirators met in a dark room. The men pulled ballots from a hat. It was determined that the man who pulled the red ballot would be designated as the killer. The conspirators were sworn to secrecy to not reveal what color ballot they had drawn. My agents learned that in order to insure that the deed would be done and the assassin wouldn't lose his nerve at the last minute, eight red ballots were placed in the hat. Each man who drew a red ballot thought that he alone was chosen to kill Mr. Lincoln. This insured them Mr. Lincoln would be killed even if one or two of the assassins missed or lost their nerve. The choice of deadly weapon was left solely up to each assassin."

Mr. Pinkerton paused, to let the news sink in. No one spoke. In fact, I don't think anyone was even breathing at that point. We were all stunned.

I looked at Mr. Lincoln for some expression of fear or anxiety. I saw none. The others in the room, on the other hand, seemed extremely concerned. They whispered amongst themselves, as if not wanting Mr. Lincoln to hear them.

"You must change your plans, Mr. Lincoln," Mr. Pinkerton insisted. "You cannot go into Baltimore at the time that has been published." Mr. Pinkerton's face grew redder and redder as he built up to the crescendo of delivering the "doom and gloom" of his message. Looking directly at Mr. Lincoln he finally said, "Sir, you have no choice."

While Mr. Lincoln thought about what the detective had said, I signaled for Mr. Pinkerton to come out into the hallway. He followed me out of the room.

Pinkerton's information, along with the report I had received earlier from Colonel Sumner, both gathered independently, had convinced me that something was amiss in Baltimore. I needed to let him know what other information I had.

"Colonel Sumner and General Winfield Scott have also come up with information of a sinister plot involving Mr. Lincoln's safety as the train approaches Baltimore," I informed him. The detective, who seemed not too interested in whatever I had to say, tapped his finger on the window ledge he was leaning on as I continued. "I will try to convince Mr. Lincoln that we need to change our plans. But, Mr. Pinkerton, I must tell you. As a man who knows Mr. Lincoln better than most anyone, he is very unlikely to be persuaded to accept any change in plans. His schedule allows him to be seen by anyone who wants to. He is adamant about not disappointing the people. And he is not trusting of anyone who he does not know. That means he certainly does not believe you."

"Listen mister," he shouted, moving toward me and shaking his fist at me. "Don't think for a minute you have any say in this matter. You're just a thug who is riding on the president's coat tails. I am the professional here — and don't you forget it."

My ire was rising by the minute, as this so-called detective got a little too close for my comfort. "Back off, Pinkerton," I insisted, pulling my six foot two frame to its highest extensions and dwarfing him. I puffed out my chest for good measure. I let my coat fall open so he could see my Colt 44 pistols. I cocked my fist and aimed squarely at his face. He backed off.

"You could be fabricating this whole story to make a name for yourself and to insure that your detective service gets more business in the future," I continued. "But I don't have time to check you out. I am in a position that I have to believe you. And I don't like to be in a position, ever, where I have no choice. We will alter the plan — but it will be my plan and Mr. Lincoln's plan — not your plan, Mr. Pinkerton! If you value your face, you will march back into the room and follow my lead." And with that I walked back into the room with Mr. Pinkerton following behind like a little puppy who had just been spanked.

Mr. Pinkerton spoke directly to Mr. Lincoln again, urging him to change the route of the train or its schedule. The detective further argued that no one outside the room be told of the plan in Baltimore, as he did not trust it to be shared with anyone else.

Mr. Lincoln asked "What would the nation think of its president if I missed a scheduled visit to Baltimore?" But then he held up his hand, not allowing anyone to answer the question.

He shook his head slowly back and forth. "I refuse to change my schedule. I have important engagements in the morning," he said with resolve. "I will raise a flag over Independence Hall. I am scheduled to speak to the Pennsylvania state legislature in Harrisburg later that afternoon. I vow to carry through on both of those commitments under any circumstances, even if I meet with death in doing so."

And then Mr. Lincoln signaled to me that he wanted to talk. We went into another nearby room to discuss the troubling situation.

"I am not comfortable with that man Pinkerton," he announced. "He seems arrogant and self-serving. I don't trust him. What is your impression, Hill?"

"I have no use for him either, sir," I admitted. "But we don't have a lot of options here. You can believe him or not. I think, regardless of our personal feelings for the scoundrel, his information cannot be ignored. We cannot take any chances with your safety."

"You are right, Hill. What are your suggestions?"

"At the moment sir, I have no plan. But I will have one for you in few hours," I promised.

"I will change my schedule at your suggestion, Hill," he reluctantly agreed. "I trust you. You develop the plan and tell me what I need to do."

We returned to the next room to confront Mr. Pinkerton and the others. Mr. Lincoln spoke first. "I will agree to get away quietly after the events in Harrisburg. I will need to tell

Mrs. Lincoln. It is likely she will insist that Hill Lamon be the only one to go along with me," he explained, pointing to me so that Mr. Pinkerton would know who he was assigning to the task.

Mr. Pinkerton grunted. "That man," he said, pointing to me, "should not be the one to accompany you, sir. I have trained men who ..."

Mr. Lincoln interrupted before the discussion could go any further. "That point, Mr. Detective, is not negotiable."

"If you want Lamon, then Lamon it is, sir," detective Pinkerton agreed. "He wouldn't have been my choice. I think you can do better, sir."

Mr. Lincoln, as usual, was quick to stick up for me. He moved right up in Mr. Pinkerton's face, looking down at the small detective and yelled, "But it's not your choice, Mr. 'So Called' Detective. It's my choice. There is no better choice than Hill Lamon. I trust him with my life. Is that so hard for you to understand? I don't have any reason to trust you or anyone you would choose for me. I go with Lamon, or I don't go at all."

"It's your call, sir," Mr. Pinkerton said, shaking his head from side to side to indicate his displeasure.

"That's right, Pinkerton," Mr. Lincoln retorted. "It is my call. I have made my decision. Good day!" And with that he left the room.

The rest of us agreed before we left that no one else was to know of the impending problems in Baltimore.

Mr. Lincoln raised the flag on the morning of February 22 (George Washington's birthday) in Philadelphia and spoke to the huge crowd at Independence Hall.

When our train left Philadelphia, we had a one hundred and six mile trip to Harrisburg, the Pennsylvania capital. The trip was projected to take about four and a half hours.

Along the way, Mr. Lincoln asked me to sit with him. We sat in silence much of the way, before he finally wanted to discuss the looming Baltimore possibilities. He hit me with a barrage of questions.

"Are we doing the right thing? Do you really believe

there is a Baltimore plot? What will the people in Baltimore think when they come out to see the president and the train arrives without me?"

"I think we are doing the only thing that is vigilant for the situation, sir. We have received information from two independent sources, coming in separate directions, of something sinister being planned in Baltimore. Our best information," I insisted, "is that the scenarios are highly possible. We should do most anything that we can to avoid placing you at risk. If either Sumner or Pinkerton had come to me with the plot, I would have had my doubts. But with both arriving at the same conclusion separately, who am I to argue?"

I continued to plead my case. "The avoidance maneuvers are not cowardly, but prudent and appropriate responses to information received from persons who were trained to find out such things. In my experience, sir, it was often the one who avoids trouble who lives the longest. Besides," I reminded him, "Baltimore has the reputation of being the northern city with the most southern sympathizers."

"I am uncomfortable with disappointing the crowds in Baltimore," he replied. "I find it dishonest to tell them they can come out to see me and then not show up. But I will follow your lead, because you have only my best interests in mind. When you have the plan ready, tell me what you want me to do and I will do it."

Upon arriving in Harrisburg, Mr. Lincoln spoke to the Pennsylvania legislature.

With that completed, my concentration focused first on getting Mr. Lincoln out of Harrisburg without being detected and then to sneak him through Baltimore in the middle of the night. The plan called for me to meet Mr. Lincoln at the Jones Hotel in Harrisburg at six o'clock, remove him secretly by carriage from the hotel and onto a nearby train. The president's train would remain on the published schedule so that no one would suspect that Mr. Lincoln was not on board.

I received Mr. Lincoln's approval of the new arrangements. And then I showed them to the detective. "Here's the plan," I told him brashly. "Take it or leave it. You don't get a vote."

"This will work," Pinkerton admitted. He didn't look very happy about the plan. "I will do what is required of me to help you."

I didn't respond. I didn't need to. He knew he had been put in his place. He knew I was running the show. He was probably disappointed that he would only have a minor role in the plan.

At the designated time, when Mr. Lincoln finished his evening meal at the hotel, a signal was flashed to him. He quickly grabbed his coat and hat, and stepped outside.

The people at the hotel were told that Mr. Lincoln had suddenly been taken ill.

I helped him climb into the carriage I had arranged. I provided him with a light felt hat he could draw down over his face and a shawl to provide some sort of simple disguise. I told him to hunch down, and to try to look shorter.

At a most inopportune time, when I was about to climb into the carriage, Colonel Sumner arrived and insisted he was going with us. At the last possible moment, Mr. Judd grabbed and pulled the surprised Colonel Sumner toward him, giving me the instant I needed to jump into the carriage and leave the premises. I was told later that Sumner was furious that Mr. Judd pulled him away. Colonel Sumner had thought he was going with us.

About that time, telegraph wires were cut in all directions from Harrisburg so no messages could leave the city. Our confidants locked Mrs. Lincoln in the hotel room, as we thought she might compromise the secret journey into Washington.

I drove quickly to the railroad station. I don't think anyone saw us as we boarded onto a special Philadelphia, Wilmington and Baltimore Railroad train consisting of only one car and the locomotive. We traveled to Philadelphia. I sat across from Mr. Lincoln on the seat, comfortable that we had fooled everyone at this end of the escapade, but uncertain as to the success of our secret journey as we got closer to Baltimore.

My disguised partner was neither comfortable nor happy. Mr. Lincoln grunted, "This is ridiculous, Hill. I look like some little old lady."

"That's the idea, sir. No one looking for the president is going to pay any attention to an old hunched over woman wearing a shawl."

"You'll pay for this embarrassment, Hill. You mark my words."

At that point, I really didn't care what the cost would be. The plan was working so far, and that was what was important. I am sure Mr. Lincoln was probably evoking some unmentionable names for Mr. Pinkerton and the situation, as I certainly was.

We both knew Mr. Lincoln was far too dignified to be dressing like a woman and sneaking around. But under the circumstances, I was doing the best I could. I told him that he needed to remain as quiet as possible. He grunted again, but then was silent the rest of the trip.

The remainder of the trip scared me, but I didn't share that with Mr. Lincoln. So many things could go wrong. We were without escort and virtually alone. I did not know if all the men in that room in Philadelphia could be trusted. I was certain Mr. Pinkerton had told all his agents – which could number as many as a dozen. Railroad officials along the way had to know this was a special train passing through, although they could not be certain its purpose. And even in watching Mr. Lincoln wearing a hat and a shawl, and walking bent over, he still didn't look much like anything but a very tall man trying to disguise himself.

Detective Pinkerton met our train in West Philadelphia at 11:00 p.m. with a carriage. Thomas Scott of the Pennsylvania Railroad and Samuel Felton of the Philadelphia, Wilmington and Baltimore Railroad arranged our transfer, and then cut the telegraph lines in the Philadelphia area.

Mr. Pinkerton drove us on a circuitous route to the city's

other train depot. The detective didn't say anything to either of us, which I took as an indication that he was doing a slow burn and trying to quell his anger with me. A berth in a sleeping car of the express train had been set up for Mr. Lincoln.

The plan was for the train to be detained until Mr. Litsenburg, the conductor, received a package addressed to "E.J. Allen, Willard's Hotel, Washington." That was the signal that Mr. Lincoln and I were on board. Litsenburg was impatiently awaiting his package as his train was already behind schedule.

Mr. Lincoln and I entered the train by a rear door. Under the guise of arranging accommodations for a sick passenger, I helped Mr. Lincoln into a sleeping berth and closed the curtains. I told Mr. Lincoln to rest and keep his shawl over his head in case someone looked in. I laughed to myself, in closing the curtain, knowing full well that the "patient" was in a sleeping berth made for a man about a foot shorter than he was. His ride in sick bay was not going to be a comfortable one.

When Mr. Lincoln was tucked safely away, the package was delivered to Mr. Litsenburg and the train was underway within minutes. Once again we were virtually alone. There were no armed guards. Even a small band of marauders could have captured the train. Mr. Lincoln may have been trying to relax at this point, but I couldn't. I was all that stood between him and disaster.

We traveled first to Havre de Grace, Maryland where the train was taken across the Susquehanna River by ferry. This was a worrisome spot for me. There were too many variables here that I had no control over. The railroad had posted guards on the ferry. I was not sure of their reliability or professionalism. Fortunately, we passed through without incident.

We arrived in Baltimore at the Calvert Street Station just about half past three in the morning, almost ten hours before our publicized arrival time. I cautiously peered out of the windows. It looked like the town was dead asleep. No one was waiting there for us.

I held my breath as our train car was pulled separately along Pratt Street through Baltimore's downtown to the Camden depot. We were hooked up to the Baltimore and Ohio Railroad engine and set out for Washington. The train passed through Baltimore completely undetected. I said a little prayer of gratitude.

We traveled to Washington City, arriving safely a 6:00 a.m. on February 23.

We were taken to the Willard Hotel on Fourteenth Street by a carriage arranged by Mr. Lincoln's friend, Elihu Washburne. At the Willard, Mr. Lincoln entered the ladies' entrance and was led to his room.

I sent a telegram to Samuel Felton of the Philadelphia, Wilmington and Baltimore Railroad informing him, "Your package has arrived safely and has been delivered."

When the regularly scheduled Lincoln train reached Baltimore at the publicized time, a large crowd of over 10,000 surrounded the train cheering in support of Jefferson Davis and the Confederacy. At that point they had not realized Mr. Lincoln was not on board.

When they finally discovered he was not on the train, hecklers pounded on the car windows, frightening Mrs. Lincoln and her sons. Railroad security drove them off. The transfer to the Camden depot was accomplished without further incident.

After the safe arrival of Mr. Lincoln in Washington, detective Pinkerton called me aside. "Lamon, I think you are a brainless, egotistical fool who has the president hoodwinked into thinking you might actually protect his life," he added, with a smirk that I wanted to physically and permanently wipe from his ugly face.

By this time I was tired and getting angrier by the minute. "Pinkerton, you listen to me," I said, while at the same time grabbing his wrist and bending it back in a very unnatural position. He was wincing in pain, but paying better attention than a man of his status might have been paying without the "incentive" I was offering his wrist. "I may be a brainless, egotistical fool, but I am also perhaps the only man capable and willing to lay down his life for Mr. Lincoln. And I could certainly break you in half without even trying. If you have any questions, now is the time to bring them up. I have a question for you, Mr. Detective. How's that wrist of yours doing, you gutless wonder?"

"And another thing, before you go. Your hair-brained scheme of assassins lurking in Baltimore to kill Mr. Lincoln was pure poppy cock. Even though we all jumped through hoops and acted as fools to sneak through the city, I have found no substantiation to your reports of a conspiracy. Mr. Lincoln does not believe there was any plot either. Perhaps you should go into another line of work, since being a detective doesn't seem to be your cup of tea."

He tried to answer, but I think the pain was overwhelming his sense of duty to communicate. I released him. The last I saw him he was muttering something under his breath as he walked away while at the same time trying to return circulation to his wrist to get it functioning properly again.

I did not tell Mr. Lincoln of my latest encounter with Mr. Pinkerton, but I was sure Mr. Lincoln would have supported my efforts to break Mr. Pinkerton's wrist.

Weeks later the president said he regretted the midnight ride into Washington that had become such a sore point in the newspapers. "I think, Hill, I made a grievous error in believing the detective's reports. I am horrified by articles in the newspaper that I had dressed like a woman to fool the people in Baltimore. I felt shame and mortification in running from the imaginary danger. I think the time called for dignity and composure, and I exhibited neither."

I could not refute any of his thoughts on the matter. But I was more relieved that we made it unharmed than I was concerned over what the reporters had to say.

My confrontations with Mr. Pinkerton brought a smile to my face every time the president made a comment about sneaking into Washington.

Allan Pinkerton, detective

Chapter 14

One of my first duties after securing Mr. Lincoln's safe arrival into Washington was to aid Benjamin French as assistant marshal of the Inaugural events, including the Inaugural parade and ceremony at the Capitol on March 4, 1861.

It was exciting for me to help Mr. French plan this very important celebration. The task was enormous, as groups interested in participating in the parade had to be sorted out and slated into the lineup. And dignitaries' egos had to be judiciously considered.

Mr. Lincoln had told Mr. French that he trusted me emphatically, and indicated that whatever assignment he gave me, I would perform well.

"Lamon, you are in charge of the safe arrival of the president to and from the Capitol. Figure out what you need to do, and then report to me with your plan," Mr. French instructed me.

I liked the job as it was similar to the responsibilities I had on the train trip to Washington. Only at the nation's capital, I had many more resources at my disposal including the Union army.

General Winfield Scott had told me he had received over three hundred threatening and hostile dispatches regarding the Inaugural events. We discussed the matter of security. "I know as well as you do, Lamon, that there are all kinds of characters in Washington who might disrupt this event. And it will take just one to make a mess of things, if he gets close to the president," the general said.

"I assume you have checked these threats out. Are you comfortable that I have assigned guards in front and back and beside the carriage carrying President James Buchanan and Mr. Lincoln? " I asked.

"The armed guards around the carriage are necessary.

We will post military units before and after the carriage, and order regular cavalry units to ride into each intersections prior to Mr. Lincoln's arrival there. We also will send troops along the route, position sharp shooters in the windows, and deploy two artillery batteries at the Capitol in anticipation of possible violence. I don't think we can over react. I have always prescribed to the theory that it is better to be safe than sorry," General Scott reported.

"I am concerned with the Inaugural speech. People can get extremely close to Mr. Lincoln from the steps of the Capitol," I warned. "What can we do there?"

"Those people will have to be in place hours ahead of time to get close. I will have thirty armed military personnel in uniform and in civilian clothes by nine in the morning to get placement up front and keep an eye on things."

"General, I think we have all the basics covered. Thank you for you vigilance in this matter."

Mr. French, having not been in the discussions with General Scott, at first questioned me on the security precautions I had planned for the event. "Lamon, you are overcautious and silly in ordering out all these military units."

"I am not asking your approval, sir," I announced confidently. "The military guards are a necessity, based on confirmed threats. The arrangements made by General Scott and myself have already been approved by Mr. Lincoln." Reluctantly, Mr. French concurred with the plan.

At precisely twelve noon, President James Buchanan arrived by carriage at the Willard Hotel to take Mr. Lincoln to the ceremony.

The Inaugural parade included their carriage. I rode my horse, watching closely for anything requiring our attention. As usual, I was fearful of the possibilities, even though I thought we had done just about everything we could possibly do to insure the president's safety throughout the event.

Around 1:00 p.m., the Honorable E. D. Baker, United States senator from Oregon introduced Mr. Lincoln in the Senate chamber to both senators and members of the House of Representatives.

Mrs. Lincoln, her three sons and a slew of her relatives sat in the gallery of the Senate, watching the proceedings.

First, Vice President Hannibal Hamlin took the oath of office.

And then everyone walked outside where thousands awaited below on the Capitol steps to watch Lincoln's Inauguration and listen to his long awaited Inaugural address.

Mr. Lincoln looked very uncomfortable in his new suit, new hat, and ebony walking stick. When he rose to give his prepared remarks, he didn't seem to know what to do with the hat and cane. He leaned the cane on the railing, while looking for some place to set the hat. At the last minute, Stephen Douglas, who he had debated throughout Illinois, saved him an embarrassment by offering to hold his hat.

Mr. Lincoln then eloquently read his Inaugural speech. I stood just behind him and surveyed the crowd. I spotted several of General Scott's men standing facing the crowd.

And then Roger Taney, Chief Justice of the Supreme Court, swore Mr. Lincoln in as President.

A tear ran down my cheek. I brushed it aside before anyone could see it. It was a tear of joy that few people could have understood.

Growing up in Mill Creek, Virginia, I could have never imagined even being invited to such a prestigious and important event. Yet not only was I invited, I was one of the men in charge, and stood just a few feet from the President of the United States — my good friend, Abraham Lincoln. It was almost beyond belief.

As I turned to leave, Mrs. Lincoln caught my eye, smiled and nodded. She was just giving the "I told you so" signal to me. I remembered the conversation we had a dozen or so years back in Springfield when she had made the amazing prediction that Mr. Lincoln would be President of the United States someday. It was amazing to me that she had accurately predicted that so long ago.

Following the ceremony, Mr. Lincoln and his wife were

taken by carriage to the White House for dining and the Inaugural Ball.

After the festivities, I lay on the floor outside the presidential bedroom, armed to the hilt, with my usual arsenal of weapons to protect the president. I barely slept, as I was still worried the day could end in violence.

One newspaper didn't let the Inaugural procession go by unnoticed. They reported seeing "a giant, garbed in a coat of military cut, with two pistols and a bowie knife in his sash of red, mounted on a splendid horse in the center of the guards in the rear of the vehicle." The vehicle they were describing was the carriage in which Mr. Lincoln and President Buchanan rode to and from the Capitol. The heavily armed "giant" dressed to the hilt the newspaper described was me.

Chapter 15

There was no time for Mr. Lincoln to learn the ropes of being President. From the moment of his Inauguration, he was immersed in the crisis at hand. He talked to me about the situation on a daily basis.

"I am as untried as anyone at national affairs," he admitted. "I have no experience in international matters. I know few proven politicians, and those who have the most experience probably would not be willing to help me anyway. I fear I am not the man for the job, but it is too late to pull out now."

"Mr. President, I think you were elected not so much for what you know, but for the confidence and trust that the people have that you are the right man for these times," I suggested. "And I know you are a man of honor and will charge ahead. You are not a quitter."

"As usual, your words are comforting. I have noticed in my life," he continued, "whenever there is a major decision to be made, it seems there is some guiding force I can't quite put my finger on that appears to help me just at the right moment. Let's hope that force remains with me through all this."

Trouble was already brewing in the South, and Mr. Lincoln needed to find out for himself what the latest developments were.

He knew that Major Robert Anderson, commander of the South Carolina harbor forts at Charleston had received instructions from President James Buchanan in December of 1860. President Buchanan had told Major Anderson to hold the fort at all costs, and if attacked, to defend himself to the last extremity.

The South had been assured by Mr. Seward that Mr. Lincoln would not reinforce Southern forts and in particular, would not re-supply Fort Sumter. Mr. Seward, a Cabinet

..iember, had sent the message without the president's knowledge.

Mr. Lincoln had chosen a policy of maintaining federal authority and not tolerating any interference. He intended to reinforce Fort Sumter at all costs.

Obviously, the positions were in direct conflict with each other.

General Scott told the president on March 12 that a larger force than he could muster was needed to fortify Fort Sumter. His recommendation was to abandon the fort.

On March 15, Mr. Lincoln polled his Cabinet. All except Montgomery Blair were in favor of evacuation.

Meanwhile, Major Anderson wrote Mr. Lincoln and told him that the men at Fort Sumter could only hold out a little while longer. He said his supplies would run out in about another month.

The morning of March 16, the president called me into his office. "Hill, I need you to travel to Charleston, South Carolina under the guise of meeting with the postal authorities concerning the movement of the U.S. mail," he explained.

"Your actual purpose is to gather information. You will be dealing directly with South Carolina's Governor Francis Pickens. I think you can help me find some kind of solution to our problem there. You will be my eyes and ears in Charleston, but you are not to speak for me. Do not make promises to any officials in Charleston or the troops at Fort Sumter."

He told me the extreme importance of the fort. He insisted, "If Major Anderson evacuates Sumter, I shall have to evacuate the White House."

I assured him that I understood his instructions. "You can count on me, sir."

I arrived in Charleston by train on March 24. My visit was not as secret as I had originally thought. I read in the next day's edition of the newspaper, the *National Intelligencer,* "Colonel Lamon arrived yesterday from Washington." The newspaper called me the "great goliath from the North." I wondered who had alerted them about my visit.

Upon leaving my hotel to walk to my meeting with Governor Pickens, I was astonished to find hundreds of onlookers watching me, like I was some circus side show. As I passed by, I was insulted by both men and women who hurled curses and epithets at me not fit to report here. And none, I assure you, were at all in the form of a compliment. I had done nothing to deserve the rash treatment other than being a "Yankee Lincoln hireling." Perhaps they thought that was enough to have warranted their abuse.

Governor Pickens met me in the hotel dining room where he and his wife had just finished breakfast. I had anticipated that we would just sit and carry on a conversation about the situation at Fort Sumter. I could not have been more wrong in my expectations.

Instead, he told me quite bluntly, "Nothing can prevent war except acquiescence of the president of the United States in secession and his unalterable resolve not to attempt the reinforcement of the Southern forts. To think of South Carolina remaining any longer in the Union is simply preposterous. We have five thousand well-armed soldiers around this city. All the states are arming with great rapidity. This means war with all its consequences. Let your President attempt to reinforce Fort Sumter, and the tocsin of war will be sounded from every hill top and valley."

Obviously, I was surprised by his comments and had no reply that I could think of off the top of my head that might be appropriate. It was apparent that Governor Pickens didn't think diplomacy was a give and take proposition. I started to respond. "President Lincoln is willing to…" but was interrupted.

"Excuse me, Colonel Lamon. Maybe I didn't make myself clear," the governor stated. "Your president can choose – evacuate the fort or he will have started a war. There is nothing to argue about or attempt to negotiate."

"Mr. Lincoln trusts me to bring your message back to him, sir," I said, adding "I would like to visit Major

...nderson at Fort Sumter."

"I will gladly arrange not only your transportation there and back, but I will also provide an escort," the governor said.

"Sir, I am capable of visiting myself, without an escort."

"That may or may not be the case, Colonel Lamon. Regardless, if you want to visit the fort, you will be accompanied by Colonel Duryea," Governor Pickens insisted. "Your choice."

"I will accept your escort," I admitted, realizing, of course, that the governor did not trust me to go on my own. And then he issued me a pass allowing for my visit.

Colonel Duryea and I were put on board the steamer Planter and transported across the harbor to the fort.

During my meeting with Major Anderson, Colonel Duryea stood off to the side, but in the same room. I found Major Anderson quite fretful of the situation.

"I am in quite a quandary, Colonel Lamon," he insisted, "unless the government in Washington reinforces the fort. We cannot last here much longer. I am frightened by the situation, even though my men are spoiling for a fight. Our position in the center of the harbor is quite tenuous. We watch troops position themselves on all sides of us. I have only about eighty-five officers and men. We would have to surrender in a month if not a shot were fired, because we would be out of food."

"I will pass the information directly to the president as soon as I returned to Washington, Major Anderson. I am certain Mr. Lincoln will act quickly to remedy your position."

I was discouraged myself, when I returned to shore. I sarcastically thanked Colonel Duryea for his assistance and then went directly to the hotel. There I was confronted by another gang of curious spectators.

A foul-smelling, seedy old man threw down a rope in front of me. He asked, "Do you think *that* is strong enough to hang a damned Yankee hireling?"

"Sir," I replied, trying to contain my irritation, "I am a

Virginian by birth, and a gentleman, I hope, by education and instinct. I was sent here by the president of the United States to see your governor."

He was quick to attack, adding quite loudly, "Damn your president."

"You, sir," I continued, resolving to stay calm but having a difficult time controlling my anger, "are surrounded by your friends – by a mob. You are brutal and cowardly enough to insult any unoffending stranger in a great city that is noted for both its hospitality and chivalry. Let me tell you that your conduct is cowardly in the extreme. Among gentlemen, the brutal epithets you employ are neither given nor received."

As the mob became even more unsettled, my friend the Honorable Lawrence Keitt arrived just in the knick of time and exclaimed, "Why Lamon, old fellow. Where did you come from? I am glad to see you."

Before I could say anything, the old man yelled, "Keitt, do you speak to that Lincoln hireling?"

Mr. Keitt was quick to respond. "Stop! You insult Lamon and you insult me! He is a gentleman and my friend. Come, Lamon, let us take a drink."

With that, we departed and the mob dispersed. I thanked Mr. Keitt for saving me from the unthinkable. Following the drink and some friendly conversation, I returned to the capitol to see Governor Pickens to ask for another pass — this time to visit the postmaster.

I reported to back to the governor, thanking him for his personal escort. He may have assumed that my comment was genuine, but it wasn't. I did not share my thoughts on how my meetings went with Major Anderson. He issued another pass, this time requesting that no one interrupt my official business with Mr. Huger, the postmaster of Charleston.

I met for several hours with Mr. Huger. After completing my business at the post office, I returned to Washington by train. And then I reported to the president on my trip. "Sir, the fort is in dire need of either reinforcement or evacuation," I said. "Major Anderson cannot hold out.

ernor Pickens made it very clear that any attempt on your part to reinforce Fort Sumter will start a war." He listened intently but did not comment. I was sure he was not comforted by my report.

Mr. Lincoln gave the order on April 4 to send provisions to Fort Sumter. The President told me he thought if the South blocked the supplies, he could deem their actions provocative. If the South fired first, they would be responsible for beginning the hostilities. I actually think that was part of his plan.

On April 12, at 4:00 a.m., the shelling of Fort Sumter began. Mr. Lincoln's supplies had not yet arrived at the fort. After withstanding the cannon fire for almost thirty-four hours, the garrison, commanded by Major Anderson, surrendered. The war had begun. It was exactly thirty-nine days after Mr. Lincoln's Inaugural address.

The night of April 13, Mr. Lincoln and I discussed the shelling of Fort Sumter.

"I sent supplies to the fort, Hill, but they were blocked. Major Anderson did not get them in time," he explained. "Now we have a war on our hands. I don't think it will be of any great length. Just the same, I will have to call up troops as early as tomorrow morning."

"I hope my trip had some value for you, sir. I found Governor Pickens rather supportive of the idea of having a war. He said they were ready for it. Are all the Northern states willing to provide troops for the cause?"

"We will soon find out."

The next day, President Lincoln called up 75,000 federal troops and ordered them to defend the Union.

On April 17, the Commonwealth of Virginia seceded from the Union. I was disappointed with the vote in my home state but not surprised. My allegiance was with the Union and not with Virginia.

Chapter 16

The president appointed me to be the U. S. Marshal of the District of Columbia. I was to serve four years through Mr. Lincoln's term of office. I would report directly to him and serve at his discretion.

"Being marshal, Hill, is the perfect position for you," Mr. Lincoln suggested. "It will allow you to be host at the White House for all events. It will give you authority over the federal prisons, and will provide you with an adequate salary. And it will keep you close to me, within arms length, if I need you."

I was sworn in on April 12, 1861. Ironically, that was the same day Fort Sumter was attacked.

My office was set up in Washington City Hall. My duties included protecting the federal courts, judicial officials, and trial participants, investigating and apprehending fugitives, ensuring the safety of government witnesses, and maintaining the custody of all federal prisons. That last task included transporting and feeding the prisoners as well as maintaining the facilities where they were incarcerated. I would execute court orders and warrants and manage any properties confiscated during an investigation.

I thought certainly the salary would be adequate by my wife Sally's standards, if I could ever convince her to actually move to Washington. I was sure the new position would keep me in the limelight, where I was most comfortable. It didn't sound like too difficult a job. I enthusiastically welcomed the assignment.

In Washington, the federal prisons under my direct control included the famous Old Capitol Prison. When the British burned the capitol in the War of 1812, Congress used this building as the capitol for a short period of time. That's where it got its name.

With the war just starting, the Cabinet searched around

Washington for accommodations large enough to house prisoners. The Old Capitol was chosen, due to its convenient location and because it could be converted from its boarding house days into a prison facility with relatively minor physical changes. The government removed a fence outside, added bars to the windows, changed a few locks, and the transformation was completed.

The prison's thick brick walls and narrow windows were a plus, but the building itself was a very broken down, dilapidated structure with old creaking doors, dark dingy interior, broken windows, and rickety stairways. The cells were filled with lice and bedbugs. The prison, located along A and First Streets, was set up to hold Confederate officers captured in battle, political prisoners, blockade runners, traitors, Union deserters, spies and smugglers.

I had thought being U. S. Marshal would be a relatively quiet and non-controversial position, even though Mr. Lincoln warned me the job would put me in a position where I would be attacked.

"In interpreting the laws as written," Mr. Lincoln predicted, "you will receive much adverse criticism and a good deal of downright abuse from members of Congress. This is certain to come, Hill, but it will be not so much intended for you as for me. As our friend Senator Hale said in the Senate the other day, 'We must not strike too high or too low, but we must strike between the wind and the water. The marshal is the man to hit.' And I say we shall have to be able to withstand whatever they send our way."

He was right. From my first day, political opponents of President Lincoln targeted me with immense pressure and agitation.

Radical Republicans in the Senate, who had voted against my confirmation, feared my strong influence on the president. They bitterly criticized my handling of the position as marshal on almost every single issue.

As part of my duties I had to enforce the fugitive slave act. This meant arresting slaves who entered the District of Columbia and holding them in jail, mostly for their own protection. At one point, I confined two hundred eighteen slaves in a prison ordinarily built to hold only fifty prisoners.

The senators were irate, announcing "When the northern states find out that they are supporting a jail for the slaves of the people who are fighting against us – and we are keeping those slaves, at the public expense, until the war is over, it will have a tendency to enlighten some minds."

Irritated Congressional leaders passed resolutions for what they called "a contemptuous restriction of its rights" and insisted that Mr. Lincoln dismiss me. Since they could not prove I actually violated any statute, Mr. Lincoln informed them he would neither accept my resignation nor dismiss me from office.

The radicals snooped on my jails frequently, trying to find some reason to criticize me and embarrass the president. To thwart their nosiness, I instructed the guards to admit only those visitors who had an official pass. Members of Congress were not issued passes. My reasoning was sound – it would insure the safety of both the prisoners and the visitors. Of course, the Congressmen who had been turned away protested vehemently.

Their personal attacks continued almost on a daily basis during my first year as marshal. I feared Mr. Lincoln was cornered, having to answer to Congress on the one hand, and having to defend me on the other. It was a situation where if he leaned either way he would be criticized.

At that point I decided it would be better to resign than continue to embarrass Mr. Lincoln.

And I wrote the following:

> January 31, 1862
> Washington D.C.
> A. Lincoln, President, United States:
>
> Sir,
>
> I hereby resign my office as marshal for the District of Columbia. Your invariable

friendship and kindness for a long course of years which you have extended to me impel me to give the reasons for this course. There appears to be a studious effort upon the part of the more radical portion of that party which you placed in power, to pursue me with relentless persecution. I am now under condemnation by the United States Senate for doing what I am sure meets your approval. By the course pursued by that honorable body, I fear you will be driven to the necessity of either sustaining the action of that body or breaking with them to sustain me, which you cannot afford to do under the circumstances.

I appreciate your embarrassing position in the matter, and feel as unselfish in the premises as you have ever felt and acted towards me in the course of fourteen years of uninterrupted friendship. Now when our country is in danger, I deem it but proper, having your successful administration of the Government more at heart than my own pecuniary interests, to relieve you of this embarrassment by resigning that office which you were kind enough to confide to my charge. In doing so allow me to assure you that you have my best wishes for your health and happiness, for your successful administration of this government, the speedy restoration to peace, and a long and useful life in the enjoyment of your present high and responsible office.

> I have the honor to be
> Your friend and obedient servant,
> Ward H. Lamon

Not surprising, the president refused to accept my resignation. "Hill, you are not going anywhere," he advised me. "The radicals will have their day, but in the end, you serve me, not Congress. Do not break under the pressure they intend for me. Do not take their assaults personally. Besides, it is not up to you to decide when you are no longer needed here. I will let you know if that day ever comes."

His loyalty and trust in what I was trying to accomplish was gratifying. But the job did not get easier

Shortly after that, the radicals voted to take away my authority as the prison warden.

I got a little revenge when two prisoners, Jeremiah Hendricks and Emanuel Pollard, were sentenced to be executed. Mr. Lincoln had appointed the new warden, but the Senate had not confirmed the appointment.

"Mr. Lincoln," I said, "I have no authority to execute any prisoners. That responsibility is part of the job description for the new warden. Remember, the senators took that job away from me."

Attorney General Edward Bates agreed with me. His ruling stated "the marshal no longer has any duty or lawful power to execute any sentence of death upon any man imprisoned in the jail of the District of Columbia."

Mr. Lincoln gave me my instructions. "Since you have no jurisdiction in these matters," he announced, winking to me on the side, "I hereby commute the sentence of both men to life imprisonment."

While I cheered his excellent handling of the problem, Congress did not appreciate his decision at all. They were angrier than they had been before. The last laugh, at least in this situation, was on them. But that didn't last long.

Congress retaliated and I ended up being their target again. The Senators set my salary for the following year at a maximum of $6000 with no additional fees. That was significantly less than my $30,000 as a marshal which had included expenses for feeding and transporting the prisoners.

It seemed that wherever I went in Washington, there was someone willing to try to weakening my position relative to Mr. Lincoln.

The president explained, "Those attacks were sent toward you to get under my skin. Congress is afraid to directly confront me. It is easier for them to attack you, Hill, because they see you as being a close ally to me. You have become a constant target."

Congressman Kellogg of Illinois attacked Mr. Lincoln. "I demand that Lamon be replaced," he insisted. "He is a disgrace as a federal marshal and a thorn in the side of Congress. You must appoint someone new right away, sir."

The president stood behind me through all of my difficulties. He told Congressman Kellogg, "You fellows at the other end of the Avenue seem determined to deprive me of every friend I have who is near me and whom I trust. Now, let me tell you, sir, Lamon is the most unselfish man I ever saw; is discreet, powerful and the most desperate man in an emergency I ever saw or expect to see. He is my friend and I am his. As long as I have the great responsibilities on me, I intend to insist on his being with me. I will stick by him at all hazards."

And I didn't complain because I couldn't defend myself -- but rather I complained because the threats took time and energy I'd have rather spent on doing something more constructive.

Even Mr. Lincoln's friends were critical of my closeness to the President. They called me everything from "a pig with a foul mouth" to "a cheating, lying rascal." Others informed him that I was not to be trusted as I was "loose cannon." Mr. Lincoln's defense of his association with me was simple. He said "It's been my experience that folks who have no vices have generally very few virtues."

And with each name I was called, Mr. Lincoln just laughed. He knew who I was. To him I was just plain old Hill, a jovial companion, a reliable bodyguard and his trusted friend. He knew I had the devotion and loyalty to never let him down. I was reliable as the day was long. The president depended on me. He called me his "particular friend."

Old Capitol Prison
Where Supreme Court is today

Chapter 17

While I was in charge of the District of Columbia jails, I was overseer of all prisoners, including several interesting female spies.

Belle Boyd, one of my most infamous prisoners, was also from Mill Creek, Virginia, where I grew up. Her family operated the general store. Her father was the postmaster for several years.

She was quite a few years younger than I was, so our paths didn't cross until we met at the Old Capitol Prison. But Miss Boyd's reputation had certainly preceded her. She was a rebel legend, having reportedly shot dead a Union soldier who threatened her mother in their house a few years previous to our meeting. Another time she was said to have ridden a horse into the parlor of their house.

Belle demanded special attention in the prison, having pretty much her own way. My guards didn't want to get close to her. I think they were afraid. She was belligerent and bold, flying the Confederate flag right out her cell window. She hung a portrait of Jefferson Davis in her cell and wrote an inscription below it, "Three cheers for Jeff Davis and the Southern Confederacy." We never did figure out how she got the flag or the portrait into her cell. She was heard singing "Maryland, My Maryland" a rebellious song when the prison was quiet at night.

After a while my guards determined it was easier just to leave Belle Boyd alone than to confront her. I'm not sure how she did it, but Miss Boyd established some kind of signals within the prison walls. Under her direction, the prisoners knew what was happening sometimes before I did.

After hearing reports of her misbehavior on a regular basis, I knew it was time for me to talk to Belle Boyd. I entered her cell one afternoon to encourage her to follow the established prison procedures, or face stern disciplinary measures. The guard who unlocked the door announced, "A visitor for Miss Belle Boyd."

Her cell, like most of the others in the prison, was not fit for human occupation. It was dark and damp. Smells of urine and mold permeated the air. There were cots in some, moldy mattresses in others. The conditions were deplorable, but it was all that I had. Her cell was large, perhaps as big as 17 by 20 feet, and was occupied by a half dozen prisoners.

As I approached, she stood and turned to face me. She was an attractive lady who looked more like a starlet than a spy. She wore a fashionable dress, though it was tattered and torn. I could not imagine how long she had worn it. She looked quite ragged and dirty. Yet somehow she reminded me of a lone light in the muck that surrounded her.

"I am Ward Hill Lamon, ma'am, also from Mill Creek, Virginia," I said, offering to shake her hand.

"I have heard of you, Lamon. I am Belle Boyd, Benjamin's daughter. I am pleased that you would visit me here in the jail," she stated. "I am normally not allowed visitors."

"This is an official, not a social visit. I am the U.S. Marshal and this prison is under my jurisdiction," I announced. "I am here to see if we can come to an understanding about your behavior while incarcerated in this facility. My guards complain that you are not following the rules of the prison."

She seemed surprised but not intimidated in any way. "Hmmm, you are a Yankee traitor, Lamon. Mill Creek's a southern town. How'd you end up on the wrong side of the war?"

As outrageous as her accusations were, I found them rather laughable. "Calling me a traitor, Miss Belle, is rather like the pot calling the kettle black," I suggested. "Look around. Aren't you the one who is in my jail?"

"I'm merely here temporarily," she insisted. "I have information I think your president, who started this war of northern aggression, might think is embarrassing to his administration. When he sees it, I think he will send me back home again."

"You will have to take that up with him, ma'am. I wish you well. In the meantime, if there are any more complaints from my guards, I will move you from this spacious cell to solitary confinement. I do not think that you will find those accommodations quite as attractive as these." I started to leave.

She couldn't let me have the last word. "I hear three of your brothers are fighting for the Confederacy. At least your mother raised a few boys with some sense."

That indeed was a sore spot for me and she knew it. My mother had written me about my brothers joining the Confederacy. I had talked to Mr. Lincoln about it, but was not comfortable that this young lady knew. It raised my ire.

I stopped and walked back toward her. "My family's personal business shouldn't concern you. In fact, the war in general shouldn't concern you. If you had kept out of it, you wouldn't be my guest here. You are charged with spying. That is a serious offense. Your time might be better spent praying that someone will take mercy on your pitiful soul. You will find no such compassion from me. Good day, Miss Boyd," I said, and walked out. The guard locked the door behind me.

I was impressed by her spunk. Miss Boyd was going to be very difficult to keep under control while she was in prison. It didn't seem like there was any quitting in her.

Much to my surprise, in late July, 1862, my friend, Mollie Pultz, was arrested and brought to the Old Capitol Prison. Mollie too had been accused of passing information to the Confederates about Union troop movements near Mill Creek. She was charged with treason, a felony punishable by death. The normal punishment was hanging.

In thinking back, my memories of her were quite vivid. Mollie was both a neighbor and a school mate. Her father's land was right alongside our farm. Many years ago, when I left for Illinois, Mollie predicted she would come back into my life someday. That someday seemed to have arrived.

In school, Mollie was really bright. She had won three school spelling bees in a row, introducing me to words I hadn't known how to spell like "camaraderie" and "juxtaposition" from Webster's book. She was very mature for her age and quite pretty too, with brown eyes that I thought gleamed like nuggets of gold. She had long dark brown hair.

Mollie was fair skinned and had a shapely figure. Her spirit was effervescent. She had a real keen sense of humor. She was also ready to break all the rules -- which surprised me for a girl. That, of course, was one thing that attracted me to her.

She didn't get in trouble as often as I did, but then no one else did either. Somehow she was better at mischief than I was because she didn't ever get caught.

Her mother and father, like most of the other parents, insisted that she find other friends and stay away from Hill Lamon. But she was just as adamant that we be friends forever.

And we made this pact, when I was in eighth grade, to do just that.

My earliest recollection of her was noticing that she followed me home from school one spring day. Each time I looked over my shoulder, she was about twenty paces behind me. I became curious as to why she was there.

Before long I was taking round-about ways to get home, dodging through the forest, back and forth across Mill Creek several times when I knew she wouldn't be able to get across without getting wet. I was on the one hand trying to lose her, while on the other, trying to test her ability to track me. Darned if she didn't keep following me all the way home almost every day.

One day I scurried over the top of a hill quickly so she couldn't see me. And then I hid in the brush. Mollie crested the hill, out of breath, stopping only a few feet from where I was hiding. She looked from side to side, trying to figure out where I had gone.

I stopped, held my breath, watched and waited. She was baffled. The young lass had no idea what happened, except that she seemed to think I had disappeared.

I waited and waited. Each minute I hid was more difficult for me than the one before. But I was enjoying the thought that she was confused and frustrated.

She sat down on a log. I snuck up behind her. I was so quiet she didn't see me until I was within a step of her.

When she finally noticed me, she jumped up, and turned to confronted me. I thought she would scream and run -- but instead she just looked at me and started to laugh. "Hill Lamon," she giggled. "You only caught me because I wanted to be caught."

"You may be right. You are Mollie Pultz, aren't you, daughter of Nicholas Pultz, my neighbor?"

"That's right. Now, what are you going to do with me?" she challenged.

Actually I didn't know the answer to that myself. "I just want to know why you are always following me," I said.

She smiled, and without hesitating, announced, "You, Hill Lamon, are the only interesting boy in the whole school."

"Why in the world would you say that?" I asked, finding a spot to sit on a nearby stump to continue the curious conversation.

"Every one in school is always talking about you -- how you are boldly playing tricks on everyone and driving the teacher crazy. They wish they had the courage you have," she explained. "I think I'm made of the same stuff as you are. I ain't afraid of no one, not even you, Hill Lamon."

"Well," I said, "I'm surprised at your persistence in tracking me. However, if you are going to follow someone, you need to learn to be less conspicuous. Next time you get captured might not be as pleasant as this time."

"I wanted you to know I was following you," she pleaded. "I wasn't trying to hide. Anyone can track and be noticed. I can track someone without them knowing I'm around."

"I doubt that," I laughed loudly. "You're just a girl."

"For a girl, I can track better than most boys. I can prove it. Give me another chance and you will see," she begged.

"What's in it for me if I let you try again?" I wanted to know.

"If you catch me, I'll quit bothering you -- but if you don't catch me, we're partners," she said.

As dumb as that idea sounded at first, I really was curious to see if this girl did have the same stuff she claimed I had but that no one else at school had. It was not that I had any idea what that stuff was, because I didn't. I thought for a moment, and then suggested, "You have a deal. If you can follow me home tomorrow without being seen, and can tell me where I had been when I get home, you can be my assistant."

She jumped up excitedly, and announced "It's a deal. And I'm betting by tomorrow at this time, we will be partners." With that she ran back over the hill and left me wondering what the heck I had just agreed to.

I was equally sure that tomorrow would be her last day of following me -- though deep down inside I was kind of hoping she had the spunk to succeed.

The next day after school I took the most elaborate round-about route home ever. I planned my route in school and was excited to get started. I forded back and forth across Mill Creek four different times, and climbed through the most desolate part of the forest where there were no trails at all. I even doubled back all the way to school. Every once in a while I glanced over my shoulder inconspicuously trying to find some sign that my feisty neighbor was tracking me.

By the time I reached the cabin, I was pretty much convinced that she had forgotten all about our little wager. I figured I was making all the deceptive moves for nothing.

Much to my surprise when I arrived home, she was sitting on the porch. "Nice try, Hill, but I tracked you all the way home."

"I don't think so. What route did I take?" I asked with delight, almost positive that she hadn't followed me at all.

As she described my travels across Mill Creek time and time again, through the dense forest, back to school, and then to the cabin, I was dumbfounded. I don't know how she did it, but she had tracked me all the way home, sight unseen. I was speechless, not even able to congratulate her for her amazing feat.

"I've heard tell that you are a man of your word," she said in a confronting smirk. "When do I start as your assistant?"

I had no choice. "Right this minute," I announced. And then I added "You certainly are made of a different sort of stuff than any of the girls and most of the boys in school. I am proud to have your assistance."

And while I had absolutely no idea what it meant having her as my partner, I had indeed made a bargain. She certainly won the bet fair and square.

Mollie was about the most determined young lady I had ever met. Even at her young age, (she was a couple of years younger than me) she was both brazen and fearless.

She challenged Mr. Hughes, our teacher, in school one day. He had insisted that all bears were carnivorous. She told him that the koala bear, from Australia, was actually not carnivorous, but was a vegetarian and had a pouch like a kangaroo.

Mr. Hughes embarrassed her in class, leading a chorus of laughter that made her quite angry. When she brought a book to school the following day supporting her notions about the koala bear, Mr. Hughes had to apologize. I don't think any of the other girls in the school would have challenged our teacher like that.

Mollie and I talked about school, church, and the town of Mill Creek. I showed her all my old newspapers and let her read them.

We dreamed aloud of the bigger world out there somewhere way beyond Mill Creek and its environs. She too was not willing to settle to have her dreams fenced in by Mill Creek. The whole world awaited us.

As I continued my mischievous and daring ways, Mollie somehow always avoided letting my exploits splash onto her. Even as a partner, whenever I got caught, she would stand innocently beside me. No one ever blamed her, even when it was her idea, her plan, and her intent. She maintained her innocence mostly because she was just a girl.

"Mollie was in the wrong place at the wrong time," I would argue whenever I got caught. "She just arrived the minute I was caught. She's just a girl. I wouldn't have let her help me set the trash bucket on fire." Then I'd wink to her and she'd get off without punishment. Actually, in that instance, she had been the one who lit the fire in the bucket.

It got to the point I would have fought anyone to the death to protect Mollie's honor, though I had no such loyalty to my own sister, Anna. It wasn't that I didn't like Anna. But she was my sister.

There wasn't anything I didn't share with Mollie. She insisted I teach her how to smoke cigars. I thought several times when her face turned green that my cigars were going to kill her. "Damn, Hill, these are awful. Why would anyone want to smoke them?" she asked as she choked and coughed.

"Parents and teachers hate the young ones learning how to smoke," I told her. "And girls are forbidden to smoke." That reason alone made her want to learn to smoke in the worst way. She survived the initial coughing and got quite proficient at smoking those retched cigars.

And then she insisted I teach her all the bad words the older boys had taught me. She practiced shouting them loudly when we were out in the woods by ourselves so that she would get the right attitude in her pronunciation.

By the third year of working together, Mollie Pultz was as bad as I was, or maybe even a little worse. I was actually thrilled at the influence I had in her life, but perhaps I had overstepped my bounds. If her parents had found out all we did, she would have been banned for life from my presence.

In those latter years, when we were alone in the deep woods, we explored each other in ways I had never experienced before. Initially we simply kissed, slowly at first, then holding the kisses longer and longer.

"Bet ya I can hold our kiss longer than you," she insisted, sticking out her tongue at me to tease me about it. And being always up for a dare, I took her challenge.

"Bet you can't," I said eager to prove her wrong.

We kissed for what seemed like an eternity. Finally I needed air and broke the lock of our lips. She won. But she also gave me ample times to try to even the score.

We skinny dipped in the pond. And then, without putting our clothes back on, we explored each other, inch by inch, touching slowly and deliberately until there was no place on either of our bodies that was left undisturbed.

Those first few times she was much bolder with her fingers and hands than I was. "You have a nice body for an older boy," she joked adding that I was "hard in the right places and soft in the right places." She slipped her hands all over my sensitive skin. As we got together more frequently, and with more encouragement from her, she taught me to explore her gently with my hands too.

I don't know what was more pleasurable for me; what her touches did to me or enjoying what response my hands raised in her.

There were times like that in the woods that I forgot about everything else, including fishing, riding horses, or playing my banjo. That's because I was enjoying so much being with Mollie.

It got so that when my family couldn't find me, they knew at least I was with Mollie, and assumed I was behaving. They could not have been more wrong.

The last time I had seen her was fifteen or so years ago, back in 1847, on the day I left Virginia to move to Illinois. She thought I was taking her with me. When she found out I was leaving her behind, she was furious.

"Dammit, Hill Lamon," she screamed. "All this time, we've been planning our escape from Mill Creek. We were going to be married. Now you are leaving me here alone, you no good son of a bitch. I'll bet this has something to do with that "hussy" Angeline Turner you've been sneaking off to see over near Shepherdstown. Bet ya didn't think I knew about her, did you?" With that she started beating on my chest with her fist, trying not to cry, but with furry and tears in her eyes.

"You are a no good bastard, Hill Lamon. It will be a cold day before I ever speak to you again. I hope you get some dreaded disease like the clap and die a lingering death before you go straight to hell."

She continued to swing her fists at me, and went on with her tirade. "Mark my words, you may leave me behind, but this is going to be the sorriest day of your life. And someday, when we meet again, you will get down on your knees and beg my forgiveness."

I was determined to get in a few choice words myself. "We never talked about being married. That was you talking, not me. You are just a spoiled little girl. This is the first time in your life that you are not getting your way. Stay here in Mill Creek and grow up. I need to move on."

Now, as I awoke from day dreaming, my first love was being held as a Confederate spy. What surprised me more than her being charged was that she had been caught.

I decided it was time to talk to her. Guards took me to her cell and opened the door. Inside the very dark and dank compartment, I saw a ragged looking lady. I called her name. She rose from a bench amidst the filth and walk towards me. Smells of the sewer permeated the air of her cell. Her clothes were soiled and torn. Her hair was caked with mud. She was dirty and haggard looking.

"Hill Lamon, is that you?" the lady whispered in a voice barely audible. "I heard you were in Washington with the Lincoln administration."

"Mollie Pultz, by God, you look a fright. What are you doing here?" I asked.

We embraced, holding on to each other silently for several minutes. And then she started to laugh. "I have been charged with helping the Confederacy by passing correspondence between the lines. Can you believe that?"

I couldn't help but laugh along with her, although the situation was not amusing at all. "Too much influence from your neighbor, Belle Boyd, I suspect," I answered, knowing full well that of all the people I knew, Mollie Pultz was certainly believable as a spy. "What happened?"

"It's not a very exciting explanation," she began. "Mother and I were attending our usual Sunday church services at Payne's Chapel. When we got on our horses to return home after church, about a dozen Union soldiers rode up and took me into their custody. Upon searching my person, they claim to have found a letter with information concerning Union troop movements they said I was carrying to the Confederacy."

"The soldiers let me keep my horse," she continued, stroking her dirty, straggly hair I had always thought was so beautiful. "I rode with them to Charlestown where they held me overnight. The next morning two armed Union soldiers took me to Harpers Ferry where we boarded the train to Washington. I think you know the rest."

"You have put me on the spot, Mollie Pultz," I explained with some embarrassment. "Did you know this was my jail? As the U. S. Marshal of Washington, prisoners in jail here are my prisoners, and my worry. Now what am I going to do with you?"

"Why don't you just let me go? I'll go back to Mill Creek and all will be forgotten."

"It's too late for that now, my friend," I admitted. "You have been arrested and charged with spying. I can't just let you out. It's not as easy as that. In fact I don't think there's anything I can do. I'm sorry."

She nodded as if she understood. I excused myself and left.

After thinking about the matter or a couple of days, I decided that I had let Mollie down before and regretted it. Now that I had an opportunity to make things right, I need to do better. I decided to return to her cell and offer another suggestion.

She seemed surprised to see me back so soon. "Do you have news, Hill?" she asked.

"I owe you more encouragement than I had given you when I was here before. I have decided that will speak to President Lincoln on your behalf," I said. "He appointed me and I answer directly to him.

I cannot make any promises."

"I trust you, Hill Lamon, as an honorable man that I know you are. I am certain you will do the best you can," she replied, as the cute smile that I remembered started to emerge from her face. "I am just lucky this is your jail and not someone else's. I will await your return with the news of my fate. And thank you for returning and trying to help me." She embraced me and then turned and walked to the rear of her cell.

As I walked out, the guard locked the door. And for a fleeting moment I imagined the troubling image of Mollie's pretty little neck with a noose around it.

I needed Mr. Lincoln's help. And I needed it now. Action would be much easier before any trial and a sentence that might need to be commuted.

Belle Boyd
Confederate Spy

Chapter 18

I went to visit President Lincoln at the White House. "Mr. Lincoln, I have a troubling situation at the Old Capitol Prison. I have a friend who has been arrested as a spy. I need you to intervene."

"I can't believe, Hill, of all the people in the world, you now have an old friend incarcerated in your jail and charged with helping the enemy. Who is this friend you are holding?"

"Sir, our new prisoner is Mollie Pultz, my friend from back home. My first love," I told him with some reluctance. Mr. Lincoln fidgeted uncharacteristically while listening to my explanation. "Mollie has that same spunk that I have, sir. You may remember I mentioned her name when you were talking about Anne Rutledge."

He nodded indicating that he did remember me telling him about her.

I paused, embarrassed for having to bare my soul. I argued that "Mollie is no different from those others that you told me you admired because they were willing to risk what they believed in for a cause, even if the cause was the Confederacy. She was probably bored at home and looking for an excuse to put her nose into a situation where a girl's pretty little nose doesn't belong."

Mr. Lincoln listened as he paced the room like a caged tiger, with his hands behind his back. And then he stopped and he sat at the table, not saying a word, and not looking at me. He was silent for a long time, leaning on his elbows, and scratching lightly at his temples in contemplation. He looked everywhere without looking directly at me.

My hands were sweating because I was uncomfortable. I really did not know what he was going to do in this instance.

"Bring her here, Hill," he finally demanded. "I would like to talk to her myself, in your presence."

I sent a message to the Old Capitol Prison, along with a

horse and buggy for her transportation. Mollie was brought to the White House under escort of three armed guards. I smiled thinking that three guards was a bit much for guarding a lady, while thinking at the same time, if Mollie wanted to escape, surely three guards would not be enough to catch her.

Upon her arrival, she reached for my hand. I led her to meet Mr. Lincoln. I was grateful someone at the prison had helped clean her up. She looked like a lady going to a party rather than a prisoner of war. She wore a long pink dress with polka dots. Her hair looked clear and was arranged in a large red bow.

"Mollie Pultz," I said, "this is President Abraham Lincoln. He asked to speak to you."

"Mr. President," she said politely, extending her hand and curtseying slightly.

"Marshal Lamon speaks of your unlawful spying escapades that have landed you in our prison," the president explained. "And he has told me that for some time you were his loyal and trusted friend. Can you see why I am having a problem with such a dichotomy, Miss?"

"Indeed I do, sir. Both of Hill Lamon's descriptions are accurate. And he will probably also explain, if asked, sir, that my only crime was in getting caught."

I nodded. "She is right, Mr. President," I offered with a slight smile. "She was a legend back home. She never got caught."

The president looked at me, but did not respond or smile. His gaze returned to our pretty young prisoner.

Mollie continued. "Sir, my trial will be held soon. I do not think your court will find me guilty, but I am responsible for my own behavior. I am just sorry to have involved my friend in my current troubles."

Mr. Lincoln looked at both of us and shook his head. And then he suggested that she remain in the room, while he and I discussed the matter in the adjoining room.

We went into the next room. "Hill, I can't believe you have put me in this compromising position," he complained.

"This friend of yours was working against the very Union I am trying to save." He shook his finger at me as if it were my fault she was here. His face reddened, and his Adam's apple bounced up and down.

His scolding continued. "Her crime is inexcusable and treasonous. And now you want leniency for her, I suppose. We should hang her in a public execution to set examples for all the other women so we can encourage them to stay home and keep out of the war. Her crime goes against everything we are trying to accomplish."

I was speechless. I had no legal argument to supporting my request. I looked at him, and then I looked down.

"Well, say something, Mr. Federal Marshal," he insisted.

"I apologize, Mr. President, for the trouble I have caused you in this instance. But I need your help," I stammered. "You have known me for many years, and have always supported me. You know I would not come to you if I knew how to handle this situation myself. You have saved me before, but never under these unusual circumstances."

"What are you asking for her?"

"A pardon, sir."

"Of all the years we have been together, you have always served me well. And I don't think you have ever asked me for anything in return. Not once have you suggested that I intercede, or grant any favors. I think in this instance, and just this one time, I owe you a favor," he admitted. "Let us return to your friend and I will tell you both at the same time what I am going to do."

We returned to talk to Mollie. She looked calm. By contrast, I was a bundle of nerves. I was still not sure what the President was planning. "I will remand this spy into your hands. You are free to release her to some reputable person back home with assurances from her and her guardian that I will not see this lady in my prison again. If she returns, there will be no second pardon. And, Mr. Lamon, we will not speak of this person again." With that he turned and walked out of the room, slamming the door behind him.

Mr. Lincoln had never even once called me Mr. Lamon.

But I was grateful for his decision.

Mollie ran to me and crushed me with a long embrace. I held on to her longer than a married man should, enjoying every second. "Thank you, Hill Lamon. How can I ever repay you for what you have done?" she asked.

"I want to apologize, Mollie," I insisted, breaking her hold of me but extending my arms to hold her hands in mine. "I said some awful things to you when I left Mill Creek without you. I have regretted that moment for all these years."

"Regretted what you said, or regretted leaving me behind?" she asked, pulling herself even closer and looking right into my eyes as if she could read my mind.

"Yes," I said smiling, avoiding the question and leaving a small doubt she could chew on later.

"And I am sorry I used every bad word that you had taught me in my anger that day," she admitted. "I have wished all this time that I could tell you how sorry I was for my behavior in that instance."

That episode being finally settled, Mollie and I talked over this new dilemma. We decided there was probably one man, Mr. Hughes of Mill Creek, our former teacher, who knew us both and who might agree to accept the responsibility of taking her home. He would have to sign an agreement to ride herd on her, keeping her under his thumb and guaranteeing her best behavior.

I asked Mollie to return with the guards to the prison to await word from me. And then I sent a telegram to Mr. Hughes asking for his help.

The following morning Mr. Hughes answered my summons saying he agreed to my proposition and was arranging transportation to come to Washington.

Two days later he arrived around noon at the prison. We met. And then I delivered Mollie into his custody. Mr. Lincoln had signed the pardon as promised. After assuring me again that she would not get into any more trouble, Mollie was free to return to Virginia.

She said she was grateful that Mr. Lincoln was lenient.

Mollie knew if convicted she faced the death penalty, even if she thought her offense trivial. She promised me, with all her heart, she would not return to my prison under any circumstances. She also realized she owed me forever.

"I hope you realize if I see you in my prison in Washington again, you will be on your own," I reminded her.

"Thank you for helping to free me from your dreadful jail," she offered with a sound of sincerity. "I am very sorry. I have learned my lesson. Do you want to know what that lesson is?"

I was afraid to ask, but I did. "What lesson did you learn?"

"I will not get caught again," she insisted with a wink and a smile, adding "Until next time, my friend…"

With that she embraced me again, and then walked away. She held her head high, as if nothing had happened, blowing me a little kiss as she mounted the Hughes' buggy to ride back home.

Strangely I believed her remorse and knew she would not be back. I was hoping that it was because she had given up her unlawful ways. But I knew Mollie too well to believe that.

Several days later, I thanked Mr. Lincoln for his pardon of my friend, Mollie. He gave me a blank stare, acting like he didn't know what I was talking about. I didn't press the issue.

As for me, I thought about Mollie often after that little episode. She had kept her promise from years ago that our paths would cross again. I had thought at the time that it might happen – but I never dreamed it would occur in a Washington jail.

Whatever information Belle Boyd had on the Lincoln administration must have been significant. Several days after Mollie Pultz was released, I received official notification, signed by Mr. Lincoln, to release Miss Boyd too.

Mollie Pultz

Chapter 19

In the evenings at the White House often everyone else went to bed. That left the president and me free to discuss most anything. Often the topic was the continuing war. And in many instances, he talked and I just listened.

"I am outraged with my incompetent generals, Hill," he admitted. "Sometimes I wonder if they have any intent on winning. The war lingers on and on. I am very torn by the bloodshed and death on both sides of the conflict. You have seen the lines of mothers, sisters and wives who come to the White House to beg me to end the war. Their lives have been made empty by the loss of their sons, brothers and husbands."

"A man from Kentucky wrote me that he had just buried his two sons," he continued, obviously troubled by the burdens the war had brought on him personally. "He said one boy was buried in a blue uniform and the other boy in a gray uniform. The father said 'God knows which was right' but I am not sure, Hill. Which side is God on? I even wonder if there is a God at this point."

"I regret deeply all the men and boys lost and maimed on both sides. But the conflict needs to continue until the Union is brought back together."

"I am criticized because I have a son, Robert, of proper age to enlist, but who is studying at Harvard College instead," he explained. "I am asked why he is not fighting, when other boys are. I think he should enlist, but Mary disagrees. She reminds me that death has already visited the White House. Willie has been taken from us. And our personal friends, Edward Ellsworth and Edward Baker, have died in the fighting."

"What we must do, Hill, is to take my message directly to the men in battle," he decided. "I need to light a fire under my generals. Please go with me and help me convince them to fight to win."

"Yes, sir," I agreed, with a little salute thrown in for good measure. "If that is what you want me to do, I am at your service."

In October, 1862, a few short weeks after the major battle that occurred in Sharpsburg, President Lincoln and I went on a trip to Harpers Ferry, Virginia, Sharpsburg and Frederick, Maryland to do just that.

The newspapers were told the mission was to thank the soldiers of the Army of the Potomac for their continued efforts on behalf of the Union. But Mr. Lincoln confided in me that the real purpose of the trip was to chide General McClellan for his "over cautiousness" and to get the general moving again.

"My army stopped the rebel invasion into the North," he told me. "But in reading the reports, it almost seemed like we won in spite of everything General McClellan did. The rebels retreated slowly, but General McClellan did not give chase. I must confront him and insist that he get go after them Confederate rascals."

We left early on October 1, traveling via the Baltimore and Ohio Railroad from Washington to Baltimore and then to Harpers Ferry.

Upon arrival on the first afternoon, we rode by carriage to review the troops stationed on the high ridge behind Harpers Ferry known as Bolivar Heights. Bolivar Heights was a Union encampment made up of most of the Second Corps. Mr. Lincoln, Edwin Sumner, General McClellan and I walked the lines of soldiers. The president stopped to speak to many of the men. He congratulated them on their courage and valor fighting in the recent battles at South Mountain and at Sharpsburg.

President Lincoln hurriedly jotted down a note and asked me to take it the telegraph office at the foot of the hill. It was to his wife, Mary. The message said, "Gen. McClellan and myself are to be photographed by Mr. Gardner if we can be still long enough. I feel Gen. McClellan should have no problem on his end but I may sway in the breeze a bit."

We stayed overnight in Harpers Ferry at the superintendent's house nearby on Camp Hill.

We walked out onto the porch after eating. "Hill," he said, "we have to end this awful war. I am afraid General McClellan is not my best hope to do that."

"Sir, you have always known the right thing to do," I reminded him. "You have given him many chances to get the job done. As the Commander in Chief, you are the one who has to make the decision. Isn't that why we came here, to press the issue?"

He seemed to ponder that question longer than I thought he might. "You are right," the weary leader finally admitted. He looked down the valley to the picturesque setting another president, Thomas Jefferson, had called "a view worth the trip across the Atlantic." For a moment, he was lost in the beauty of the area. And then he announced, "I will tell General McClellan again what to do, and I will take action -- firm action, if, or rather when, he doesn't follow through."

On October 2, we traveled toward Sharpsburg in carriages, stopping in the areas of Loudoun Heights, Maryland Heights and Pleasant Valley along the route. Mr. Lincoln stopped at each encampment and personally thanked the soldiers.

And then we visited with General Fitz John Porter and the troops of the Fifth Corps stationed at the Grove Farm just west of Sharpsburg. From there Generals McClellan, Porter and Burnside showed us around the sites where the actual battle had taken place.

The fields of battle were quiet. The generals told of the devastation, with thousands of dead and wounded, now all buried or in hospitals. The president was feeling sad, and after returning to camp, asked me to play my banjo for him. The others joined in singing many of the silly old songs I provided as we sat around the campfire.

Tents were set up to accommodate our party at McClellan's headquarters, also on the Grove farm. The tents were not very glamorous, but in light of the accommodations the troops lived in night after night in defending the Union, I had no problem with the simple setting. Mr. Lincoln had no qualms about sleeping in a tent either. He reminded me of his days in the Black Hawk War when he slept in the cold and ate raw pork along with all the other recruits.

We laughed at the accommodations while sharing the tent, admitting that the cramped quarters in the taverns along the Eighth Circuit looked like palaces compared to sleeping here on the ground.

Mr. Lincoln could not sleep so I stayed the watch with him. "Hill, you don't know how helpful your banjo playing is in times like these. Those songs lift me out of the difficulties of the day, even for a few minutes. Thank you for providing those instances of lightness I need occasionally during these troubled times."

"It is my pleasure to serve you, sir, in whatever way is helpful."

On October 3, we were sitting around the fire eating breakfast (some concoction of mush with several bacon strips and hot coffee) when I spotted my "friend" detective Allan Pinkerton walking into the camp.

It was an opportunity I couldn't pass up. My mischievous little mind moved quickly into its "revenge" mode. As he got closer, I dumped a large handful of salt into my mush, stirred it and headed in the opposite direction to the mess tent. There I asked an aid for another serving, as a new guest had just arrived. I passed the mess aid my plate and asked him to deliver it along with a hot mug of coffee to that little man standing right over there. I pointed to Mr. Pinkerton. The soldier was happy to oblige me after I had passed him a silver coin. I waited behind a tree, about thirty yards from the action.

The detective was slow to eat, sipping his hot coffee gingerly, like a man who hadn't had a good brew in a while. He talked to several of the soldiers. I waited patiently. Finally he dipped his large spoon into the mush, brought out a nice size helping, and sloshed it into his mouth. Within seconds he was spitting it out, cursing and yelling for the lad who had brought him his breakfast. Fortunately for the soldier who delivered meal and who looked physically like just about any other soldier in camp, he had made tracks to the other side of the farm at my earlier suggestion.

Mr. Pinkerton was furious. Mr. Lincoln looked up and wondered what the fuss was all about. I was enjoying the moment beyond Pinkerton's range of observation. I walked away.

Later Mr. Lincoln caught up with me. "Did you see that commotion with Mr. Pinkerton's breakfast?" he asked.

"Twas something, wasn't it?" I answered with a snort. "I wish I had thought of doing that!"

Mr. Lincoln laughed heartily saying, "I think it caught his attention." I was pretty sure Mr. Lincoln knew who was responsible for the incident, but neither of us discussed it further.

I kept my distance from detective Pinkerton until he left the camp. I don't know if he knew I was there. But I know it certainly was worth what it cost me to have him be the brunt of my little mischief for the day.

After breakfast, General McClellan and the President left to review more Union troops including the Ninth Corps of General Burnside. A twenty-one gun salute was fired from the artillery battery announcing the president's arrival.

Upon returning to General McClellan's headquarters, Mr. Lincoln was taken into the house by Mr. Grove. His house was being used as a hospital and held battle field casualties. There the president chatted with wounded soldiers from both the Union and the Confederacy.

Following the house tour, Mr. Lincoln was brought out to review more of the Union troops, this time talking to men from the First Corps.

Back at the Grove farm, Alexander Gardner, a war photographer arrived at General McClellan's headquarters. He was scheduled to take photographs of the momentous occasion. Mr. Gardner asked President Lincoln to pose with several different groups of officials in attendance.

One was an interesting photograph that included me. Mr. Gardner insisted I be seated at the opposite side of the pose so as not to detract from Mr. Lincoln. The photographer told me I couldn't stand next to the president because we had similar top hats, black clothes and were about the same height. It was as if he thought someone could not have distinguished between the two of us. I thought it rather ridiculous that he thought we looked alike. Who was he kidding?

While on the trip, I was able to converse at length with Mr. Garrett, president of the Baltimore and Ohio Railroad. He was concerned about the railroad's role in transporting supplies to the Union Army.

Mr. Garrett told me the railroad's main line was constantly being interrupted in the vicinity of Berkeley Springs, Martinsburg and Harpers Ferry, Virginia. In these areas, the middle of the Maryland owned railroad passed through the South on its way between Cumberland and Baltimore.

The railroad president said, "In this vicinity, the Confederate Army spends most of its energy trying to keep the Virginia section of the B & O Railroad disrupted by pulling up the rails, heating them in hot fires, and then bending them into 'bow ties' around trees. The rebels blow up the bridges and tear up the tracks regularly, requiring large sections to be rebuilt to keep our trains running."

But there was more. He told me "Stonewall Jackson's men had even trapped trains in the Virginia section on May 22, 1861 and had stolen or destroyed forty-two locomotives and 386 train cars. Those they took were pulled down the wagon road by horses to Winchester, Virginia for use on Southern railroads. They also destroyed over 36 miles of track, 102 miles of telegraph wires, and burned the B & O roundhouse complex in Martinsburg."

"Colonel Lamon, I need the president's help and support on this matter," he concluded.

"I assure you that I will talk to Mr. Lincoln to see if there is something he might do to help remedy your costly situation," I said.

The trip to see the troops had caused Mr. Lincoln to be

even quieter than usual. So many men from both sides had been victims of the battles here -- the numbers estimated at around 21,000. We had been told it was the bloodiest single day battle to date in the awful war.

Mr. Lincoln asked me several more times to sing and play the banjo. He wanted a little gaiety from me. "Hill, can we have some of your fine tunes to brighten up these trying days?" he inquired. I certainly was ready to perform those songs whenever he asked.

I could tell when those times were coming on. He would sit by himself and look out into the sky. If you watched him closely, he didn't look around or connect with anything. He was just staring at nothing. He was like that frequently. I knew to leave him be, but always had my banjo handy when he requested it. I wasn't surprised after Mr. Lincoln visited the wounded and dying, it would be followed by a night of singing.

Of all my songs, Mr. Lincoln requested the silliest ones the most. He knew all the words, and more often than not, joined me in singing along, though he was totally and utterly incapable of carrying any tune at all. But that never seemed to stop him from participating.

When I sang that song about old John Brown, he sang loudest at the part that says "his truth is marching on."

After the snoring began in the tents that surrounded us, Mr. Lincoln and I talked some more.

"Hill, I really admire that these men all are willing to risk their lives to save the Union. Even the ones in the hospital, missing arms and legs, and others blinded by shells and barely clinging to life, reached out to touch me as if I had been sent to save them."

"I'm no savior," he insisted. "I'm just a man like they are. In fact, they could easily blame me for their wounds. I have terrible burdens on my shoulders, but I don't have to duck bullets in the field like they do. It seems like they are much better men than I am. I wonder if I am setting the right course of action. What do you think, my friend?"

"I too am awed by the courage of these men to stand up

to the rebel guns to save the Union," I admitted. To lighten the moment, I offered a suggestion. "Perhaps you should put those radicals in Congress in blue uniforms and march them to the front lines. Maybe they would think twice about criticizing your position." He thought that was a fine idea, and laughed heartily.

"Sir, I think whatever you do you will be wrong in some of people's eyes. The alternative is to do nothing. But as a man of honor, you cannot stand back and do nothing. You have to do what you think is best. That's all you can do. Some will insist that you didn't do enough. Others will be convinced that you did too much. Even if you win the war, sir, some will say you were wrong anyway."

He thought for a few minutes, pondering what I had said. "Hill, it is always comforting to hear things from your perspective. Of all the decisions I have made following my election, trusting you to come along with me was one of my best. Thank you for being a steadying influence on me. And for being such a good friend."

"And don't let me forget, when we get back to Washington, that I should look into a way to get those congressional radicals into some blue uniforms," he insisted.

On October 4, we passed through Sharpsburg on our way to Frederick where another train awaited to take us back to Washington.

We stopped just east of Sharpsburg at the Pry house to visit General Israel Richardson who was convalescing in an upstairs bedroom from wounds inflicted in the battle.

When we left, General McClellan provided us with a cavalry escort and rode with us to the top of South Mountain before returning to his headquarters. We passed along sites of the battle of South Mountain. We continued to Burkittsville where Mr. Lincoln stopped at several churches to visit more of the wounded men.

When we arrived in Frederick, a large crowd lined Patrick Street to get a look at the president. From there we went directly to the Frederick railroad station to board one of Mr. Garrett's trains.

Mr. Lincoln and I stood on the back of the train as we pulled out of the station. He waved slowly to the crowd, hat in hand. He continued waving until the last person in the crowd was out of sight. As he turned to come into the train car, a loud cheer rang out, as the train passed through a large encampment of Union soldiers. They were rejoicing that they too had gotten to see the president.

"Hill," he said on the return trip, "I think General McClellan is a lost cause. He often can't wait to send a telegram to me after the battles telling me he has won, yet when I read the newspaper accounts I find that we had actually lost those same battles. It makes me wonder if General McClellan was somewhere else."

Even after our trip to Sharpsburg, when the president ordered General McClellan to lead his men south, the general waited some more.

Mr. Lincoln worried about the war every waking minute. I think a blanket of grief had enveloped Mr. Lincoln. His demeanor changed. The longer the war dragged out, the more melancholy he became.

"Hill," he explained, "if I cannot end the war and pull the Union back together, I will forevermore be known as a failure. I cannot bear that." Many a night he couldn't even finish a discussion about the losses, because he was so ill equipped personally to handle the burden he carried as the nation's leader. I am not sure anyone could carry such a heavy load.

He sat often by himself, lost in thought. I think he was totally overcome by feelings of being helpless in the war situation.

Library of Congress photo

Alexander Gardner photograph
McClellan's Headquarters
Grove Farm in Sharpsburg, Maryland
Lamon is second from left, seated

Chapter 20

There came a time in early 1863 when Mr. Lincoln approached me about carving out a new state from the western portion of the large area that we all knew as the Commonwealth of Virginia.

Western Virginia, I knew, was very split on which side they were supporting in the war. The area where I had grown up, around Martinsburg and Charlestown, Virginia, were definitely Confederate strongholds. In a more northern part of western Virginia, Wheeling was a hotbed for Union activity.

Other areas of western Virginia had organized fighting units for both the Union and the Confederacy from the same town. It truly was a situation where neighbors were fighting against each other, and even in some instances, members of the same families were fighting on different sides.

After I left Virginia, I was appalled to hear that three of my brothers had joined the Confederate cause (those brothers that Belle Boyd had chided me about), while I was working to maintain the Union with the President.

Mr. Lincoln said representatives from western Virginia had met and voted to split off from the Commonwealth of Virginia into a new state to be called West Virginia.

The President explained the situation and looked to me for some comment. He showed me on the map what the new boundaries might be.

"Looks to me, sir," I suggested, "that this old Virginia boy is about to have his boyhood places fixed into the North."

"Is that a bad thing for you, Hill?" he asked.

"No sir. I don't think so. My family still lives in Virginia, so I have some mixed feelings on the matter. But with all the years I have spent in Illinois, I pretty much feel like I am a full-blooded northerner anyway."

I understood, after all the time we had spent together, Mr.

Lincoln was looking for my thoughts, not my advice. I knew he was not going to change his mind on the line dividing the states, but I appreciated that he at least asked for my comments. Soon Summit Point, Virginia, where I was born, would be Summit Point, West Virginia and Mill Creek, Virginia, where I grew up, would become Mill Creek, West Virginia.

"Having lived so long in the North and obviously helping with your administration," I told him, "I have long since abandoned my allegiance to the South. It would be an honor for my home territory to be included in this new northern state. But may I ask you why the boundary is drawn here?"

Mr. Lincoln explained he and Mr. Garrett of the Baltimore and Ohio Railroad had come together to discuss the problems of the railroad in Virginia. I had passed on to him the information Mr. Garrett and I had discussed on the Sharpsburg trip.

"The railroad is crucial to the North. As it stands now, this northern railroad crosses here at Harpers Ferry into the South," he explained while at the same time pointing to the map, "and then emerges back into the North right here, near Cumberland, Maryland."

He drew an imaginary line with his finger where the new boundary would be. The southernmost part of the new state, he showed me, was very close to my western Virginia roots.

"It would be quite helpful," he said, "to the Union cause and to Mr. Garrett to have his entire railroad in the North. And as long as you have no objections to your home territory, I think I shall approve the new boundaries as I have shown you here."

Not all agreed with the splitting off of West Virginia from Virginia including Attorney General Edward Bates who argued the move was unconstitutional.

And with the drawing of that new boundary just a few miles south of those two little towns, both Summit Point and Mill Creek became part of the new state of West Virginia, approved on April 20, 1863. It would officially become a new northern state in sixty days, on June 20.

Chapter 21

Around the first of November, 1863, I received an invitation from Judge David Wills of Gettysburg, Pennsylvania to take charge of the procession and the ceremonies at the dedication of the National Cemetery. In his invitation, Judge Wills explained that he wanted me to act as marshal of the event on November 19.

I wanted to accept the invitation but had arranged to go to Springfield at that same time to bring my wife to Washington. I was torn between my duty to the president and promises I had made to go to Illinois.

I met with Mr. Lincoln to get advice from him on the matter and showed him my invitation from Judge Wills.

"Mr. President. I have a dilemma. As you know, Sally has said she would be willing to move back to Washington if I promised to spend more time with her. I pledged to her that I would. This invitation from Judge Wills asking me to be marshal for the dedication ceremonies certainly looks important, but the date conflicts with my trip to Illinois to bring her back with me. What would you recommend I do?"

"Hill, in view of your relations with both the government and with me, you would do well to accept this important assignment," he insisted. "I will write to our friend Judge Davis from the Eighth Circuit and see if he can arrange for someone from Illinois to bring Sally to Washington. By the way, I have been invited to give a short address at the dedication."

With that little problem solved. I informed Judge Wills that I would be marshal of the day. Judge Wills told me the Honorable Edward Everett would be giving the major oration, while Mr. Lincoln had been asked to formally dedicate the cemetery to its sacred use with some brief remarks.

He shared with me that Mrs. Lincoln violently protested

his involvement in the ceremony, pleading with him to stay home as their son, Tad, was ill with scarlet fever. Mr. Lincoln said she had thrown a tantrum, screaming at him and reminding him that they were still in mourning and trying to recovering from the recent death of their son, Willie. "She told me that my duty was to her and my family. She suggested that I let the people in Gettysburg find someone else to speak at the ceremony."

"I told her that she was wrong. I insisted that on this one very important day in Gettysburg, no one can take my place. And that it is my honor and duty to attend. Needless to say she was quite angry with my decision."

I started making plans for the event. I divided the preparations into two phases: those things I could arrange from Washington and those specific plans that I needed to complete while in Gettysburg.

Mr. Lincoln and I discussed the event several times. Mr. Lincoln expressed his fears to me that as President he would not be able to deliver a speech that would fulfill the people's expectations. I encouraged him by telling him that I thought he certainly would speak well, as he usually did. He showed me ideas for his speech. He said he was having difficulty writing down the right words because this was such an important event.

I sent out telegrams to the states with soldiers buried in the cemetery, asking the governors to send a marshal to assist me with the ceremony. Twenty states appointed a representative to work with me. I asked Benjamin French, who I had helped with the Inauguration, to be my second in command.

My associates and I arrived in Gettysburg on November 12. We met with Judge Wills and then worked on the event procedure. We decided the procession was to be formed in the town's center and proceed to the cemetery along the main street. Working out from the "diamond" configuration in the square in downtown Gettysburg allowed me to line-up groups in all directions, and then feed them into the procession in quite an orderly fashion.

Mr. French told me he had written several verses for the commemoration. He was a poet, of sorts, and had taken on the responsibility after hearing that invitations to write a poem for the event sent to Henry Wadsworth Longfellow, William Cullen Bryant, and John Greenleaf Whittier had all been turned down.

We went back to Washington on November 13, returning to Gettysburg again on Tuesday morning, November 17.

I worked with all the marshals for the rest of the day finalizing the parade plan. I was concerned with the president's safety throughout the planning sessions. Judge Wills brought in extra soldiers at my request. Their orders were to march in procession along side the president's horse, to keep people away from him.

Their charge during the ceremony at the cemetery was to stand in front of the stage, facing the crowd, and looking for anything unusual or anyone acting suspiciously.

I met with the men on three different occasions, trying to help them realize that in a crowd of this size someone might be there just to cause harm. I was satisfied after our third meeting that these men were serious about their duties for the day.

All day Wednesday I met with about seventy assistant marshals at the Adams County Courthouse, discussing all the last minute details of the elaborate procession.

At six that evening, President Lincoln, Secretary Seward, and other dignitaries arrived at the Carlisle Street railroad station in Gettysburg.

By nine o'clock on Thursday morning, November 19, all the marshals had assembled wearing fancy sashes and carrying batons.

Mr. Seward and Mr. Lincoln went off with Judge Wills to take a carriage ride around the battle sites. I sent a detachment of cavalry soldiers to shadow their carriage, to assure Mr. Lincoln's safety.

The roads in every direction to Gettysburg were packed with carriages, buggies and every kind of wagon imaginable, bringing people to the ceremony. The area looked more like a county fair than a small town preparing to honor its war heroes. The noise was overwhelming.

It was almost eleven when the procession began to move toward the cemetery, a little bit later than I had hoped. We fed the assembled units out into the "diamond" like clockwork, just as we had planned.

The sidewalks were lined with thousands of people wanting to get a glimpse of the solemn procession.

The colored guard led the line of march. Two bands, the 5th New York Artillery Band and the 2nd U.S. Artillery Band, played as they marched. Amidst all the fuss, the parade moved forward like a long snake, making its way down Baltimore Street toward the cemetery.

I had caught a glimpse of President Lincoln during the procession. I was embarrassed to see that the horse someone had assigned him to ride was too small. The president's long legs almost reached the ground on each side. Oh, how I wished they had gotten him a taller horse. I was pleased, however, to see that the guards had him surrounded as he rode down the street.

He was wearing his tall hat with a mourning band around it, in remembrance of his son, Willie, who had died in February of last year. The hat band was certainly appropriate for this solemn occasion.

As the procession ended, I switched to the job of being the master of ceremonies for the dedication itself. I realized this was perhaps my biggest opportunity ever to be in the limelight. I mounted the stage and was awestruck by all the people crowding around. The amount of people in attendance was possibly more than fifteen thousand, and was spread out as far as I could see in every direction.

I was very uncomfortable for the president's safety in all the throngs of people. They crowded tightly up against the platform. On this day Mr. Lincoln could certainly have been an easy target for anyone inclined to harm him. My guards took up their positions in front of the platform.

I looked around for the Honorable Edward Everett, the key speaker of the day, but could not find him anywhere. I asked Mr. French, but he had not seen Mr. Everett either. In fact, Mr. French said Mr. Everett had not shown up for his spot in the procession. I waited and waited. Mr. Everett was nowhere to be found. I waited some more. Finally I could wait no more. I needed to get the program underway.

I gave the nod to the Birgfield's Band of Philadelphia and the music started.

When the band was finished, the prayer was offered by Reverend T. H. Stockton, the chaplain of the U.S. House of Representatives.

I myself was praying for deliverance of Mr. Everett. Where was the famous orator? I frantically put my marshals on alert around the stage to look for the man who was to give the major address. We couldn't go much further in the program without him.

While the marshals were still searching for Mr. Everett, I told the audience of the dignitaries who sent their regrets as they could not attend the event. And then I read a letter from General Winfield Scott, apologizing that his ill health prevented his attendance. Finally I recited from letters of regret from Major General George Meade and Treasury Secretary Salmon Chase.

Next I called upon the United States Marine Band to play a musical selection.

While I was listening to the music, Judge Wills came over to my chair and told me that Mr. Everett had his own tent set up behind the stage and was waiting there to be summoned. Mr. Everett had told the judge the procession would exhaust him, so he decided not to participate.

I thought to myself, "Too bad no one had informed me." I sent Mr. French to find the famous and obviously very well pampered orator to hurry him up. Mr. Everett had already put the program about thirty minutes behind schedule.

By the time it was his turn to speak, Mr. Everett climbed unhurriedly up the steps and onto the stage. I motioned for Benjamin French to introduce him.

I was so annoyed for the first several minutes of his presentation that I paid no attention at all. Who was this man who thought he was so special that he did not have to follow any of the official protocol?

Mr. Everett talked and talked and talked. After a while, I became more annoyed at the length of his remarks than the fact that he had set my program behind schedule.

He was interrupted frequently by applause. But the longer he spoke, the more restless the crowd became. By my watch he spoke for almost two hours. And then Mr. Everett finally ended his oration and sat down. The crowd gave him a polite, but not over-zealous ovation. I politely clapped simply because he was finished.

Following the main speech, the Baltimore Glee Club sang the Consecration Hymn written by my associate, Benjamin French, as he proudly listened. His words certainly did fit the solemn occasion.

And then it was my turn to introduce the President. It was a proud moment for me, both in having been marshal for the entire event, and for being able to introduce my friend, Mr. Lincoln.

My remarks didn't take long. I simply said, "Ladies and gentlemen, the President of the United States, Abraham Lincoln." The crowd gave him a rousing cheer, and then settled in to hear what he had to say. I was quite interested to listen to what he had settled on from the notes he had shown me in Washington.

Mr. Lincoln rose and strode to the front of the platform. He reached in his pocket and extracted his remarks. He put on his spectacles. The president sounded very much at ease, and seemed comfortable with his words as he spoke them.

He had told me his remarks would be very brief. And he was right. His speech was over before some had quieted down. The crowd didn't seem to know how to react. Some clapped politely, but they may have been stunned that in just a few minutes, it was over.

The photographer on the scene complained later that he barely had ducked under the hood of his camera to take a photograph of the President, when Mr. Lincoln had finished

I signaled a local choir and they sang a funeral dirge

accompanied by the Birgfield Band.

As the finale, the benediction was given by Dr. Rev. Henry Baugher, president of Pennsylvania College.

Following the benediction, I announced that the Ohio delegation would host a reception at five o'clock at the Presbyterian Church at the corner of Baltimore and High Streets.

By three o'clock, the procession had moved back to the square, following the reverse direction of the earlier march.

At 6:30, the president and his party were escorted by soldiers back to the train station, and their train departed to take them back to Washington.

After the presidential train left, the crowd dispersed. Judge Wills and I walked a block back to his house. He had ales delivered into the sitting room where he announced, "I toast you, Colonel Lamon, for a job well done."

We clanked our mugs together, and I relaxed for the first time in two weeks. We sipped the suds slowly and enjoyed the moment.

"I don't know how the day could have gone any smoother, Lamon" the judge commented.

I laughed out loud. "Perhaps if someone had told me of Mr. Everett's plan, we could have gotten back here to drink ale about an hour sooner." He joined in my laughter, shaking his head in agreement.

Gettysburg Address
Lamon seated to Lincoln's left
Lloyd Ostendorf – used by permission

Chapter 22

As the war continued on, my unofficial duties as Mr. Lincoln's bodyguard became more important. My assistant marshals and the prison guards brought reports on a regular basis of plots to cripple the government, and to kidnap or harm him.

Our sources were prisoners overheard in their cells, reports coming from an inside source in the Confederate Secret Service, from Union spies living in the South, and various others of official or unofficial capacity. And although the reliability of the information was always in doubt, I had to make sure all leads would be thoroughly investigated.

I had files on every organization and individual. Some files were extensive, while others were scant. Several names popped up over and over again. Rose Greenhow, another lady rebel spy. Michael O'Laughlin. Samuel Knapp Chester, actor. Samuel B. Arnold.

At least two men in the South were being watched on a regular basis. G. W. Gayle, had advertised blatantly in the *Selma* (Alabama) *Dispatch*. He said he would kill Lincoln, Seward, and the vice president for one million dollars and was soliciting funds for that purpose. Another southerner, Dr. Blackburn, we learned, had proposed delivery a gift of clothing to President Lincoln. Those clothes were infected by yellow fever, small pox and other contagious diseases.

The *New York Tribune* newspaper reported details of a plot they had uncovered to kidnap Mr. Lincoln and take him to Richmond. That idea had supposedly originated from the administration of the Confederacy.

I had paid informants throughout Washington, Richmond and in most areas of the South. I elicited information from prisoners by offering them larger amounts of food, or withholding rations, depending on how willing or reluctant they were to cooperate. I had even used certain diabolical means including undue force in several occasions to gather information critical to my investigations.

Mr. Lincoln surely would not have approved of my methods, but he didn't have a clear understanding of the danger he was in either.

As disconcerting as those plots were to me, I was also fearful of the access that anyone in Washington had to Mr. Lincoln on a daily basis. His office in the White House opened its doors to all comers as they requested appointments, favors, special treatment for a family member captured in the war, or whatever. Mr. Lincoln spoke to each and every one, calling their requests a "beggar's opera" and denying my suggestion to at least register each guest in a log book.

Threats on Mr. Lincoln's life were hand delivered or mailed regularly. I questioned how the government could allow such flagrant disregard for the safety of such a high official. Mr. Lincoln reminded me that even threatening letters were an expression of free speech, one of the nation's most revered rights.

I kept myself on high alert every single day. The Metropolitan Police firing range was at my disposal, and I used it on a weekly basis to hone my shooting skills. I "killed" many a paper target by blasting it with my Colt 44 pistols. My smoking guns had a calming effect on my mind. I regularly took them apart and cleaned them so they were always in tip top condition.

My knives were sharp enough to skin a cat. And I kept my muscles toned by punching a bag I hung in the basement of my house.

Many a night I slept on the floor outside the president's bedroom, arriving after he and Mrs. Lincoln went to sleep. Each night I simply rolled myself in my cloak for warmth and lay down at the bedroom door, passing the night with my small stash of weapons within easy reach. The next morning I left before Mr. Lincoln was awake. I don't think during that whole four years I protected the president he ever even knew

I was there.

One night after midnight, Mrs. Lincoln was startled when she stumbled over my body in the hallway. When I explained my presence and how often I slept at that spot, she was actually relieved. "Does Abraham know you sleep here?" she asked.

"No ma'am. And I would like that to be our little secret, if you don't mind."

"I will not tell him, Hill. And thank you being here."

After a while, I got comfortable sleeping on that hard floor. But I still woke up with any discernable noise, ready to jump into action.

Mr. Lincoln told me a story of an incident that he called an "accident" but which I would classify as an assassination attempt.

"I was returning from the Soldier's Home," Mr. Lincoln said, "when I heard a rifle shot. The horse I was riding bolted with the noise. I was fearful for my life, as much from the runaway horse than from the gunman, who I did not see."

The next morning, a man near the Soldier's Home appeared at the White House to deliver Mr. Lincoln's hat. It had a bullet hole plumb through it.

Often in the dark, I would walk around the grounds of the White House, looking for new ways that someone might gain entrance without being seen. I had a keen eye and a devious mind. I knew what my imagination might be able to conjure could also be plotted out by some diabolical character with kidnapping or assassination of a president on their mind. Mr. Lincoln received hate mail on an almost routine basis. He laughed each one off as more ridiculous than the one before, but I was not so sure.

We had both Confederate and Union troops in the capital, political friends and foes, loners, foreigners, estranged politicians, disgruntled citizens and everything in between. I didn't think it was a stretch at all to consider the worst possibilities.

The threats continued. A Cabinet member told him, "Listen to Colonel Lamon. There are evil men in

Washington. I don't think you are taking very good care of yourself. There are enough rebels here who would try to be a hero by harming you."

Mr. Lincoln responded angrily. Throwing down a packet of letters, he denied that there was any danger. "Every one of these letters contains personal threats to me. I do not have time to worry about that. I am not able to avoid all possibilities of harm."

And he didn't seem to worry about it — ever. It was my job to worry about it every hour of every day.

Secretary of War Edwin Stanton was one of the few other men in Washington who agreed with me that we needed to do whatever we possibly could to ensure Mr. Lincoln's safety. In a meeting he arranged with the president and me, he was adamant. "Mr. Lincoln, Lamon and I are privy to the same information," Mr. Stanton told us. "You need to take greater care in traveling outside the White House. I, for one, am adding a military escort to your trips to the Soldier's Home in the evenings. I am also assigning additional guards to the White House grounds."

Mr. Lincoln scoffed at the suggestions. "I see that Lamon's got you buying into his conspiracy theories too. I am surprised you support him. Your efforts remind me of a farmer in Illinois who questioned why God put a curl in a pig's tail. It didn't seem to have any use," Mr. Lincoln commented. "I think the Lord probably knew what he was doing. I don't think guards are necessary, but Mr. Stanton probably has a reason for them. As long as Mr. Stanton was in charge of that, I think the boys will continue to guard me."

One night Mrs. Lincoln was riding in a carriage from the Soldier's Home when the horses bolted, dumping her onto the ground. She hit her head and was bleeding, but was otherwise unhurt. Someone had loosened the bolts of the seat where the driver had been sitting, causing the whole seat to come loose.

Following this serious situation, I asked the Metropolitan Police to assign four more guards to the White House and to accompany Mr. Lincoln when he left the grounds. Though I had requested the help and had finally received some, I had heard rumors that at least one of those guards, John Parker, was not a reliable police officer. I took my concerns to Mr. Lincoln.

I met with the president. "I am worried about Officer Parker, recently assigned as your guard," I told him. "I have heard rumors and would like to personally check his records to establish whether the charges have any substantiation. I am told that he has been charged with conduct unbecoming of an officer, insubordination, visiting a house of ill repute while on duty, carelessly discharging his firearm, insulting a woman, gross negligence, and a whole litany of other offenses."

"Nonsense, Hill," he insisted. "My wife, Mary, knows Officer Parker personally and would vouch for his reliability. I am comfortable that he is guarding me."

I was steaming inside. I did not want to hear that the president's safety was now in the hands of Mrs. Lincoln. After all, throughout the war, the newspapers had questioned her personal loyalty to the Union.

"Sir, I must insist, this time, that I be allowed to pursue my hunches until they are satisfied," I argued with more forcefulness than usual.

"You will do nothing of the sort. This is just another of your fool-hardy measures to cry 'wolf' when there's no wolf in this hen house," Mr. Lincoln fumed. "Drop the matter, Hill."

"Yes sir, whatever you say. After all, you are the president." I stormed out of the room angrily. Under close scrutiny, I am sure steam was coming out of both of my ears. I was madder than I had been in years.

On another occasion, Allan Pinkerton, the detective who I had worked with on the train to Washington, told me of a plot by leading Democrats to harm Mr. Lincoln. His agents allegedly overheard them developing the scheme. Mr. Pinkerton demanded authorization from President Lincoln to check out the matter.

"Mr. Pinkerton, that's not going to happen," I told him

emphatically. "Mr. Lincoln did not appreciate your advice back on the train to Washington. Your information on a plot to kill him in Baltimore caused him great embarrassment. He didn't trust you then and he doesn't trust you now. The president is not going to give you authorization to investigate this matter." He stormed out. I knew nothing further would come of the matter.

My wife, Sally, continued to complain vehemently. "I wake up in the middle of the night and you are gone," she shouted angrily. "For all I know you have been at the tavern all night." Finally she got so disgusted with me that she moved back again to live with her family in Springfield. I did not like her leaving, but did not blame her either.

I could not defend myself against Sally. I am not sure why I hadn't explained to her that I left my house each night at ten and went to the White House, checking with the guards and making sure the house and its occupants were being guarded.

One night I even climbed onto the cornice of the executive mansion to see if I could get into the president's bedroom without the guards detecting me. Luckily for me I didn't get shot. They were doing their job, as they did discover me. When they found out that it was me they thought I was insane for my attempt. But I was just trying to prove a point.

Every day I tried my best to protect Mr. Lincoln, while he argued that he did not need me to be his personal bodyguard.

His disregard for my advice was maddening to me. I wanted to scream and yell at him for his carelessness. Talking to him hadn't work up to this point. I started leaving him notes.

I wrote: "I regret that you do not appreciate what I have repeatedly said to you in regard to proper police arrangements connected with your household and your personal safety. You are in danger."

When I got no response at all, I offered my resignation for the umpteenth time since arriving in Washington. As usual, it was not accepted.

Another time I wrote a letter expressing my outrage as to what I thought was the president's reckless behavior.

"Tonight, as you have done on several previous occasions, you went unattended to the theatre. When I say you went unattended, I mean you went alone with Colonel Sumner and a foreign minister – neither of whom could defend themselves against an assault from any able-bodied woman in this city. You know or ought to know that your life is sought after, and will be taken, unless you and your friends are cautious. You certainly know that I have provided men at your mansion to perform all necessary police duty. I am always ready myself to perform any duty that will properly continue in your interests and your safety. God knows that I am unselfish in this matter."

His reaction was typical. "Hill, you old fool," he said, cornering me in the hall of the White House. "Your insistence that I will be harmed by some hidden enemy is downright foolishness. For a long time you have been trying to keep somebody -- the Lord knows who -- from killing me. You see more demons than anyone I know. And they are all imaginary. We have had this discussion before. We will not discuss it further. Good night."

I tried to respond, but Mr. Lincoln put his hand up to halt me. He would not hear anything more from me on the matter.

My ire was quite aroused, but I knew better than to try to get in the last word with the president. He was in charge. He did what he darn well wanted to do, with no regard as to my suggestions even though part of my job was to watch out for him.

My "assassination envelope" alone contained over eighty

threatening letters. Secretary Stanton had told me he had another eighty-seven letters threatening Mr. Lincoln's life.

I backed off for the time being – in spite of the threat from Mr. Dubois and the men from Illinois on the train to Washington. They had put the president's health, well being and safety in my hands, under their threat to me. How had they put it? "We entrust the sacred life of Mr. Lincoln to your keeping. If you don't protect it, never return to Illinois, for we will murder you on sight."

I didn't drop my guard or stop worrying about his safety. Believe me; it is not easy to protect someone who feels absolutely no need for protection.

Chapter 23

It was quite ironic to me that in the 1864 election, General McClellan was Mr. Lincoln's opponent -- a man who couldn't make a decision in a reasonable amount of time to save his soul. Did the Democrats think suddenly the slow and very predictable McClellan would quickly change his stripes as president?

I thought that was about as likely as me giving up smoking cigars and drinking whiskey. Those things were not going to happen.

I feared a nation who would vote for General McClellan as its next president.

During the presidential campaign between Gen. McClellan and Mr. Lincoln, the newspapers published a report of an incident in 1862 when we visited General McClellan at Sharpsburg.

The report said:

> One of Mr. Lincoln's Jokes -- The second verse of our campaign song published on this page was probably suggested by an incident which occurred on the battle-field of Antietam a few days after the fight. While the president was driving over the field in an ambulance, accompanied by Marshal Lamon, General McClellan, and other officers, heavy details of men were engaged in the task of burying the dead. The ambulance had just reached the neighborhood of the old stone bridge, where the dead were piled the highest, when Mr. Lincoln, suddenly slapping Marshal Lamon on the knee, exclaimed: "Come, Lamon, give us that song about Picayune Butler, McClellan has never heard it."

"Now you please," said General (George B.) McClellan, with a shudder, "I would prefer to hear it some other place and time."

Many other newspapers picked up the report as fact and ran it in their editions. Upon reading the report, I became incensed. I couldn't believe how twisted the story had appeared, with little semblance as to what actually had happened. The accompanying cartoon was even more outrageous, showing Mr. Lincoln walking amongst men who were dead and dying.

Even though the article and cartoon misrepresented what actually happened, I had to laugh. The artist had drawn me from my best side – with only my back showing.

I took the newspaper to Mr. Lincoln. He read it silently. He thought about it for a few minutes. And then he expressed his personal outrage at the implications of the article and cartoon.

The angered President Lincoln wrote the following response as if it were written by me:

> The president has known me intimately for nearly twenty years, and has heard me often sing little ditties. The battle of Antietam was fought on the 17th day of September, 1862. On October 3, we all started on a review of the three corps, and the Cavalry, in the vicinity of the Antietam battle ground. After getting through Gen. Burnside's Corps, at the suggestion of Gen. McClellan, he and the president left their horses to be led, and went into an ambulance or ambulances to go to Gen. Fitz John Porter's Corps, which was two or three miles distant. I am not sure whether the president and Gen. Mc. were in the same ambulance, or in different ones; but myself and some others were in the same with the president. On the way, and on no part of the

battleground, and on what suggestion I do not remember, the President asked me to sing the little sad song, that follows, which he often heard me sing, and had always seemed to like very much. I sang them. After it was over, some one of the party, (I do not think was the president) asked me to sing something else; and I sang two or three little comic things of which Picayune Butler was one. Porter's Corps was reached and reviewed; then the battleground was passed over, and the most noted parts examined; then, in succession, the Cavalry, and Franklin's Corps were reviewed, and the president and party returned to Gen. McClellan's Head Quarters at the end of a very hard, hot, and dusty day's work.

This is the whole story of the singing and its surroundings. Neither Gen. McClellan nor any one else made any objection to the singing; the place was not on the battle field, the time was sixteen days after the battle, no dead body was seen during the whole time the president was absent from Washington, nor even a grave that had not been rained on since it was made.

Even after that fine explanation which I concurred with in total, Mr. Lincoln would not allow me to send the response to the newspaper. He did tell me, "You know, Hill, this is the truth and the whole truth about the affair; but I dislike appearing as an apologist for an act of my own which I know was right. Keep this paper, and we will see about it." The newspaper report went unchallenged.

I was completely puzzled as to why he would write the response, explaining what really happened, and then insist that I not send it. I confronted him about it.

"Sometimes, Hill, even when you are right," he

explained, "it is hard to get the right words of explanation so that the people will listen. This is one of those cases. This is not a twelve person jury. This is the whole American public that we would have to appeal to. They will not believe whatever we say if they choose not to. And if they know me for what I am, they will not believe the newspaper account."

"But sir," I pleaded. "You told me that even if the odds were 1000 to 1, if I was right, I needed to stand up for myself. Are you forgetting that you gave me that advice?"

He laughed. "At least you remember some of the things I taught you. Believe me, in this instance, no matter what we said we can not win the argument."

I did not understand completely, but I did take his word for it. Over the years, I had learned that his gut feeling generally was right.

I learned later that the report and cartoon was run every single day by newspapers who were trying to defeat President Lincoln.

Mr. Lincoln's re-election was certainly not guaranteed. In the last thirty years, no president had been elected to a second term. His attitude was if the people wanted him re-elected they would do so. If they didn't want him to be re-elected, he would be quite all right with that decision too. His supporters were hoping that he would be re-elected president.

In the early elections in Ohio, Pennsylvania and Indiana, the Republicans carried all three states. On that same day, Maryland adopted a new state constitution abolishing slavery.

In November, the election totals were tabulated from the other states, with the results showing a close popular vote, but with Mr. Lincoln garnering a large plurality in Electoral College votes. The vote was Lincoln 2,213,665 to General McClellan's 1,802,237. But Mr. Lincoln's electoral votes far surpassed his opponent, 212 to 21. McClellan only won the states of New Jersey, Delaware and Kentucky. Surprisingly, General McClellan didn't even get the vote from the Union army he had been expecting.

Harpers Weekly political campaign cartoon
Lincoln, Lamon (his back showing) and General McClellan
Sharpsburg, Maryland

Chapter 24

No piece of legislation captured more of Mr. Lincoln's personal attention than his attempt to pass the thirteenth amendment. The amendment was quite simple. It called for slavery and involuntary servitude to cease within the United States except for the punishment of a crime.

He worked day and night to garner support from Congress. It took much of his attention and energy. Mr. Lincoln even assigned me to twist some arms, as he knew I was attuned to that kind of exercise. I encouraged several dozen members of the legislature to take the thirteenth amendment under quick advisement at their state meetings. I emphasized the measure's importance to the president's efforts.

"Hill," he said to me. "This amendment has been needed for years and years. If I don't pass this, I will be deemed a failure."

"But sir," I insisted. "Remember years ago when you tried to free the slaves in the District? You introduced the legislation that did not pass. Don't you remember that years later the legislation was finally adopted? You have no vote in this procedure. Isn't it enough that you are supportive of its passage?"

"No, Hill," he replied. "This must pass. In fact, it must even be adopted in the South to heal the wounds brought on by the war."

He worked diligently all during the latter part of 1864 to place before Congress the amendment that would eliminate slavery, once and for all in the United States.

The thirteenth amendment to the Constitution was finally proposed to the legislatures of the states by the Thirty-Eighth Congress, on January 31, 1865. Ratification of twenty-seven of the country's thirty-six states was required to officially adopt the amendment.

Mr. Lincoln was quite proud that the first state to ratify the thirteenth amendment was the state of Illinois. The Illinois legislature met and unanimously ratified the amendment on February 1, 1865.

My new state of West Virginia ratified the amendment on February 3, and my state of birth, the Commonwealth of Virginia, adopted it on February 9.

The president had told me many times "this nation cannot stand half free and half slave. If I can save the Union by freeing the slaves, I will do it – and I will not wait for the end of this dreadful war."

Chapter 25

Mr. Lincoln returned from Richmond in the very early days of 1865, telling me that the end of the war was near. "We must prepare to unite the country, Hill," he demanded. "Many of the Cabinet members want to punish the South for secession but I will have none of that. Those states that seceded must be returned, like the prodigal son. We have to hold out our arms and accept them back with no retribution or penalty, and get on with the business of healing the Union."

On April 9, General Ulysses S. Grant sent a telegram to Secretary of War Edwin Stanton declaring "General Lee surrendered the Army of Northern Virginia this afternoon."

That evening Washington slowly found out the news of the surrender and responded enthusiastically. People flooded into Washington's street, shouting wildly, shooting off fireworks and guns, banging on pots and pans, whistling and screaming.

On April 11, thousands surrounded the White House calling on the president to speak. He spoke from the balcony, telling the people that his sole object now was to bring the seceded states back into the Union.

The war was finally over. I personally thought everyone on both sides had grown tired of it. I was surprised that it had dragged on for almost exactly four years.

Mr. Lincoln asked a band to play "Dixie" for him. "That song," he said, "is now legal property of the Union."

I noticed he was cheery, funny and in high spirits for the first time since our days on the Eighth Circuit.

We met later that same evening. "The Union has been saved, Hill. We must start, not tomorrow, but today, bringing the Union back together. We will begin what I am calling reconstruction. We cannot show any malice along the way to our brothers and sisters who yesterday were our enemies.

Today they too are Americans, just like we are. And Hill, you are to be an important part in my reconstruction plan."

Mr. Lincoln's words did not surprise me because I had been listening to his speeches all along. He was doing what he thought he needed to do to preserve the Union. Now that the Union was saved, he wanted to start, as quickly as possible, to patch it up and get it running smoothly again.

President Lincoln was looking for just two things from the South -- loyalty to the United States government and ratification of the thirteenth amendment. He was very proud that by this time, twenty states had already ratified the thirteenth amendment.

He proposed a quick reconstruction without humiliating those people who had rebelled against the government. General Grant thought the majority of the people of the North and the soldiers all favored Mr. Lincoln's stance on reconstruction with leniency toward the South.

The president said if Jefferson Davis fled without being captured, he would not be overly concerned. He worried if Jefferson Davis were captured, Mr. Lincoln would be quite unpopular if he didn't punish him.

The Cabinet opposed Mr. Lincoln's reconstruction ideas. Vice-President Johnson in particular insisted that the South's sins were enormous and the states that seceded should be severely punished. That angered Mr. Lincoln. He was harsh in criticizing the vice president, telling him that everyone must support the president's plan on this matter.

That same evening, April 11, I was ordered by the President to go to Richmond, Virginia to attend a series of meetings regarding the impending reconstruction efforts.

I argued that my place was here in Washington, standing guard, as always. But my idea fell upon deaf ears. "I need you in Richmond, Hill," Mr. Lincoln insisted. "You know better than anyone my thoughts on reconstruction. I want you to convey my plans to the legislature of the Commonwealth of Virginia."

"It is my duty, sir, more than anyone, to stay and protect you," I argued, with enthusiasm. "I am the only one who can be trusted with that assignment. With all due respect, sir, if you write out your instructions, most anyone can represent you in Richmond."

"I ordered you to go to Richmond for this important mission. And that's what you will do. Now go pack, Mr. Lamon," he insisted, quite sternly, shaking his finger at me. "And be ready to leave immediately. How dare you question my orders." He turned and walked away.

Once again, in anger, he had called me Mr. Lamon. He had only done that one other time.

I was angry and quite frustrated. I balled up my fists, ready to fight, but I knew I wouldn't use them. I smashed my hand into the wall instead, slightly injuring my hand without causing much damage at all to the unforgiving wall. I swore under my breath hoping no one would hear me.

I went home and packed a bag, against my better judgment. When I was ready to go, I asked Secretary of the Interior John Usher to go with me to help me persuade the president to exercise caution. I did not want him to go anywhere while I was away in Richmond.

We went to the White House. "Will you promise me, sir, that you will not go out at night, particularly to the theater, while I am gone?" I asked.

President Lincoln spoke to Mr. Usher as if I were not in the room. "Usher. This boy is a monomaniac on the subject of my safety. I can hear him or hear of his being around, at all times of the night, to prevent someone from murdering me. He thinks I shall be killed; and we think he is going crazy. What does anyone want to assassinate me for? If anyone wants to do so, he can do it any day or night, if he is ready to give his life for mine. It is nonsense."

I stood silently, steaming inside, but not saying a word. I knew I was right. I was torn between insisting that I be heard again, and knowing my arguments would not count. We had been down this road before. Mr. Lincoln had not changed his tune on the matter of his safety since becoming president.

Mr. Usher responded. "Mr. Lincoln, it would do you well to listen and give heed to Colonel Lamon. He is thrown among people that give him opportunities to know more about such matters than we can know."

I asked again for his promise as I grabbed my hat and got ready to leave.

"Well," the president said. "I promise to do the best I can toward it." Then he shook my hand and added "Good-bye. God bless you, Hill." And he walked away.

Allow this bearer, W. H. Lamon & friend, with ord... any baggage to pass from Washington to Richmond and return—

April 11, 1865   A. Lincoln

Copy of Presidential Pass given to Lamon

Chapter 26

I reread the telegram I had received at the hotel in Richmond again and again, hoping somehow I could change what it said.

Washington, D.C.
April 15, 1865
2:00 a.m.

Ward Hill Lamon:

President Lincoln has been mortally wounded by a lone gunman at Ford's Theater. I doubt he will survive the night. Your services are required at the White House. I have sent a steamer to bring you back to Washington. Please make haste.

Edwin Stanton
Secretary of War

I was as shocked and saddened as anyone in the world to receive news in Richmond that my best friend had been shot.

I was also angry that in spite of my insistence that he not go to the theater, the president attended the play.

The newspaper reported that Abraham Lincoln had died.

Much of the time I awaited the ship to take me back to Washington was spent going over in my mind the confrontation with Mr. Lincoln in the White House before I left. Mr. Lincoln and I had not ever been involved in such an angry argument. Now I would never get a chance to apologize. I felt bad enough that I had not been there to protect him at the theater. The guilt of spending our last moments together in conflict was almost too much to bear.

In my mind, the next several years would have been the most important in this country's history. I thought Mr. Lincoln was poised to lead the necessary reconstruction of the Union. I believed he was the absolute best man to carry on that terribly important task.

I took the steamer back to the nation's capital. Upon my arrival in Washington, a carriage with guards whisked me quickly to the White House.

We drove past people on the street moving very slowly, grieving Father Abraham, in a public outpouring I had never witnessed before. The celebration over the end of the war was already over. It had lasted less than a week. But Mr. Lincoln would have wanted it that way. He didn't want the Union to gloat over a victory — he just wanted to bind the nation back together.

The Capitol building itself and the whole city had already been draped in black.

At the White House, the scene was as somber as anything I had ever experienced. Cabinet members and staff looked out into space, not being able to even talk to each other. Tears flowed as readily as whiskey at a party.

I looked around and found stable, long-time politicians and friends who had crumbled and fallen off their lofty pedestals. Those who were always solid as a rock in any legislative crisis were the most lost. Many were unable to function at all. The colored help cried alongside the political leaders, as the invisible angel of death strangely seemed to bond them together as one.

No one wanted to talk about what happened, as if not talking about it would change the reality.

I looked for someone who might be in charge. There wasn't anyone who looked capable of taking the lead. The crisis had shriveled the national leadership to a bunch of non-responsive imbeciles. A foreign power could have overthrown the government of the United States at that moment without firing a shot.

I looked around for someone, anyone, who still had their facilities intact, but I could find no one.

John Hay, one of Lincoln's secretaries, appeared in the doorway and motioned for me to follow him. I pushed through, though no one noticed or cared. He led me upstairs to the guest bedroom where Mrs. Lincoln sat sobbing on the bed.

I knelt before her, taking both her hands in mine. I stayed motionless for several minutes not knowing what to do or say.

When I looked up, Mr. Hay pointed to the next room. I got up and walked into the adjoining bedroom and found my friend, Mr. Lincoln, stretched out on the bed, covered by a thin sheet. I gasped. I was horrified. I could not look. I didn't dare look. I would not look. I did not want to remember him like that. I fled the room in horror. In the hallway I fell to the floor sobbing out of control.

I don't know how long I cried for my friend, his widow, his family, the Union and even for myself. I cried for our friendship and for all the times we shared the best and the worst together. I cried that our last moments together had been in anger. I cried for the county's loss. And I cried that I wasn't there at the theater to possibly thwart his assassination.

Chapter 27

The next morning George Harrington, Prosecuting Attorney for the District of Columbia, called me into his office. "Hill, you are the obvious choice to organize the Lincoln funeral and the trip back to Illinois with his body. I know this will be difficult, but I am certain you will do a stellar job. Mr. Lincoln would have wanted you to personally handle all the arrangements."

I knew he was not asking. He was telling me. And he was right. Mr. Lincoln would have wanted me to have this assignment. I was not sure I could do it. But Mr. Harrington was already walking out of the room. He was not waiting for me to convince him he needed to find someone else.

My experience at the first and second Inaugural events and the procession at the Gettysburg National Cemetery did make me the best candidate for the job. I couldn't argue that.

I was proudest of this event, and aimed to make it the finest ceremony that ever took place in this country. But at the same time, this was my most difficult task.

I was so emotionally distraught by the loss of my best friend, I could barely operate. Organizing an event of this size required all my faculties. I had few under control. I could barely breathe. I could make lists. I could send messages. Planning coherently was almost beyond my grasp. But then no one around me was managing much better than I was. We were all gripped in a kind of paralyzing quicksand. We did the best we could under the circumstances.

I was inundated with requests to participate. I put out feelers to anyone who had private carriages and riding horses I could use to transport the dignitaries. Almost two hundred people volunteered to be assistant marshals, and I needed every one of them.

Many of the details of the event remain a blur in my troubled mind. I am not real sure whether I don't actually remember what happened, or I just don't want to remember. This is what I recall of the event.

The president's body laid in state in the East Room of the White House on Tuesday April 18. Thousands and thousands of mourners passed by the casket.

On Wednesday, April 19, sixty clergy and over six hundred dignitaries participated in a funeral at the White House. Mrs. Lincoln was conspicuously missing, refusing to leave her upstairs bedroom.

The casket was taken by pall bearers into a hearse. The hearse carried Mr. Lincoln's casket on the one mile trip to the Capitol. Sixty thousand or so people marched in the procession and another forty thousand watched from the sides of the street.

His body was placed in the Capitol from Wednesday afternoon until Friday morning for public viewing. Thousands more walked by to pay their respects.

It was an awesome and unforgettable site to watch. It felt like everyone had lost a close friend. Unlike most funerals, where some of the family is hysterically crying and their friends are holding them up, the Lincoln funeral was quite different. There was no one to hold anyone else up. It affected everyone profoundly. No one seemed immune from the horrendous loss people were experiencing. I didn't think the lines would ever end.

The radicals in Congress couldn't leave me alone even during the funeral proceedings. They demanded a meeting with me to explain why I had included several secessionists as parade marshals. We met. I explained my decisions. They objected. I walked out, but not before using several of the words the older students at my school had taught me – words I had almost forgotten I knew.

A better man would have walked away without the insults, but there was no better man around. So they had to deal with me. At that point they could do what they wanted to me. I had a job to finish. They did not want to mess with me further.

Those senators were very lucky I didn't have my arsenal

of weapons with me, because by the time I was through with them, I was ready to shoot and kill three or four of those trouble makers. In my state of mine, I would have thought nothing of it. In fact, perhaps if several would have been found dead, it may have improved the legislature.

On Friday morning, April 21, the remains of the president were transferred to the Baltimore and Ohio Railroad station to begin a trek back to Springfield, Illinois. The funeral train left Washington at 8:00 a.m., leaving behind a huge crowd at the station. We followed basically the same route the train had taken to bring Mr. Lincoln to Washington four years earlier.

That funeral train took us through northern towns for over 1900 miles, with memorial services and the president's body lying in state in the same cities where he had spoken at rallies right after his election.

Seventy-five thousand people greeted us on our return to Springfield, Mr. Lincoln's home.

On May 4, the body of Abraham Lincoln, my friend, and his son, Willie, were put to rest in a public receiving vault at the Oak Ridge Cemetery in Springfield.

Four others who had ridden the Eighth Circuit with him, Major General David Hunter, Secretaries John Nicolay and John Hay, and Judge Davis stood next to me as we said our final goodbyes.

I was the last person to leave the cemetery, staying after the others had left. I wanted time alone with my friend.

I was torn between screaming at him at the top of my lungs for his carelessness that got him killed – and telling him how empty my life would have been without his friendship.

"Mr. Lincoln," I said to the gravesite in front of me. "You have been the most important person in my whole life. The lessons you have taught me along the way have helped me to be a much better man that the man who grew up in western Virginia. I will be forever indebted to you for your encouragement, trust, kindness and advice. Your friendship was a wonderful gift I will cherish as long as I live. Rest, my dear friend, knowing that you finally brought peace to the Union. I hope now we can rebuild the country in your honor."

I truly did not know how I would be able to carry on now that he was gone. And I was not optimistic that the country could carry on either at this point.

Chapter 28

Washington was different when I returned from the funeral in Springfield. There was an aura of grief on every corner. The black bunting hung from the buildings, and a pall of death was draped on the people who lived here. The citizens of Washington, from the lowliest bum to the wealthiest landowner, seemed personally to have lost a beloved friend.

The short-lived excitement of having the awful war over was replaced by the squalor of an unending gloom.

I wanted to divorce myself as quickly as possible from Washington and its environs. A governorship appointment was available in Idaho. I thought that would be far enough away. I asked my long time friend, Supreme Court Justice David Davis, to write a letter to support my appointment as governor of Idaho. A fierce fight ensued in Congress over my appointment. Upon hearing of the troubles, I withdrew my name from consideration.

President Johnson urged me to become a member of his Cabinet. He offered me the position of Postmaster General. But I refused. I resigned as U. S. Marshal. This time my resignation was accepted. I received the following acknowledgment:

Department of State
Washington
June 10, 1865

To Ward H. Lamon, Esq.
Marshal of the United States
for the District of Columbia
Washington, D.C.
My dear sir:

The president directs me to acknowledge the receipt of your letter of the 8th instant, in which you tender your resignation as Marshal of the United States for the District of Columbia.

He accepts your resignation, as you desire, to take effect on Monday, the 12th instant, but in doing so deems it no more than right to say that he regrets that you should have asked him to do so. Since his advent here, he has heard from those well qualified to speak of your unwavering loyalty and your constant personal fidelity to the late president. These are qualities which have obtained for you the reputation of a faithful and fearless public officer, and they are just such qualities as the government can ill afford to lose in any of its departments.

They will, I doubt not, gain for you in any new occupation which you may undertake, the same reputation and the same success you have obtained in the position of United States Marshal of this district.

Very Truly Yours,
William H. Seward

My time in Washington was over. I need to move on with my life. It was time to reacquaint myself with my wife, Sally, and my daughter, Dolly. I never had time for either one of them before. I hoped it wasn't too late.

Perhaps, as some of my friends had already suggested, I will write a book about my adventures with Abraham Lincoln. I knew him as well as anyone.

Chapter 29

Years after President Lincoln's death, my curiosity got the best of me.

I returned to Washington and checked into the Willard Hotel, not knowing how long I would be staying.

As a former federal marshal, I was looking for some answers concerning the Lincoln assassination. Because of my federal post, I was privy to files and reports the average citizen would not have been able to see.

My investigation was certainly unofficial and more to satisfy my need to know.

I spent most of my investigation studying the duties of the guard assigned to President Lincoln when he went to Ford's Theater against my advice on April 14, 1865. The guard's name was John Parker, the man who I had urged Mr. Lincoln to allow me to investigate following his assignment at the White House in the fall of 1864.

To this day I have not been able to totally figure out how Officer Parker was chosen for this important duty. The evidence surely presents an odd set of circumstances.

John Parker, from Frederick County, Virginia, had been a Metropolitan Police Officer since 1861. Officer Parker had a troubled career, as he was charged with conduct unbecoming an officer to using violent, crude and inappropriate language, drinking on duty, verbally abusing a fellow officer, visiting a house of ill repute while on duty, sleeping on duty, general inefficiency, gross negligence, insulting a woman, and insubordination. In every instance but one, the charges were dropped. In the other incident, he was actually tried, found guilty and dismissed from the police force, only to be mysteriously reinstated eight months later.

In the fall of 1864, the Washington Metropolitan Police Department received an unusual request that this very same, less than reliable policeman, John Parker, specifically be assigned to the White House as a guard.

Upon further investigation, the story became even stranger to me. Police officials told me the request had been made by Mary Lincoln, on executive mansion stationery. She asked that another officer be replaced from the White House assignment and insisted that Officer Parker be assigned there instead. When I had questioned him, Mr. Lincoln said his wife would vouch for Officer Parker's reliability.

The thought that Mrs. Lincoln might have been involved in a plot to kill her husband made my blood boil. But what else could I have assumed from finding out this information?

I chased down various rumors of a possible relationship between Mrs. Lincoln and John Parker, but there was nothing that I could substantiate. All I know is that I saw and recognized Mrs. Lincoln's signature on the orders to assign Officer Parker to the White House detail.

All during the war, Mrs. Lincoln's loyalties had often been questioned by the newspapers. Most of her family was fighting for the Confederacy. Mr. Lincoln stood by her, fighting off the critics. I think he trusted her.

The afternoon of April 14, Mr. Lincoln, who I knew to be a shrewd judge of human nature, asked Secretary Stanton to assign Major Thomas Eckert to accompany them to the theater rather than Officer Parker. Mr. Stanton told the president that Major Eckert already had been assigned some other duty that night and could not be spared. Mr. Stanton reaffirmed Officer Parker's assignment to escort the president and Mrs. Lincoln.

At Ford's Theater, the night Mr. Lincoln was shot, Officer Parker was dressed in civilian clothes and carrying a .38 caliber police revolver. His orders "to stand there, fully armed and to permit no unauthorized person to pass into the box" were certainly clear and concise. It was an assignment even John Parker should have been able to understand.

Instead, with the play in progress, Francis Burns, Lincoln's coachman, told me that Officer Parker left his post to grab a drink at a nearby saloon. In conflicting testimony,

Parker's partner, Officer William Crook, claimed John Parker took a seat in the dress circle as he could not watch the play from the position assigned outside the presidential box.

Regardless of where Officer Parker actually went, his departure left the door to the box unguarded. A lone gunman, John Wilkes Booth, entered the box unchallenged. Booth shot Mr. Lincoln at close range in the back of the head. The assassin stabbed Major Rathbone and then leaped from the box onto the stage and fled.

To complete the strange evening for Officer Parker, he showed up at 6:00 a.m. at the Metropolitan Police headquarters after being missing the entire evening. As far as I could find, no one in the police department was looking for him. He was not even questioned when he returned to headquarters.

When I asked Officer Crook about it, he told me it was his personal opinion that had Officer Parker carried out his assignment, the president would still be alive.

Following an investigation of the events at Ford's Theater, Metropolitan Police Superintendent A. C. Richards filed charges against Officer Parker for dereliction of duty. The charges against him read: "That said Parker was detailed to attend and protect the president, Mr. Lincoln; that while the president was at Ford's Theater on the night of 14th of April last, said Parker allowed a man to enter the president's private box and shoot him."

Officer John Parker was tried on May 3, 1865. On June 2, the case was dismissed. Officer Parker was never even reprimanded, and in fact, was returned to the White House for guard duty.

When I asked for copies of the transcript, I found the court files had mysteriously disappeared. No one in the clerk's office could find the official testimony from Officer Parker's trial.

In 1868, John Parker was dismissed from the Metropolitan Police for sleeping on duty. It seemed peculiar to me that Officer Parker would be fired for that offense, and yet had no disciplinary action taken for his behavior which led to the death of the president of the United States.

And although there is no evidence that I could find that implicated Officer Parker in any conspiracy, it seems curious to me how he continued to get preferential treatment in spite of his conduct. As an attorney, I could find no argument he might have presented to justify his behavior.

In other related information about the case, I could find no listing of Major Thomas Eckert on any duty roster for that evening, although Secretary Stanton had told Mr. Lincoln that Major Eckert had already been assigned to some other duty.

I finally tracked John Parker to a house on L Street in Washington where he was living. I wanted to talk to him. I was not sure Parker would welcome me but I was convinced he would recognize me within the first two seconds of my arrival.

And I was convinced Parker would not want to be interrogated by me. I was extremely angry at him and would use considerable physical force and persuasion, if needed, to elicit some kind of explanation as to what he was doing that fateful night. In fact, I was fearful that he might not survive my questioning.

I watched the house for two days from an alley across the street, making myself fairly inconspicuous for a man my size. During the early evening of the second day, I observed Parker entering the house. I waited and then walked across the street. I bounded up the porch steps and knocked on the door, positioning myself where anyone inside looking out would not be able to see who I was.

A lady answered the door. "May I help you?" she asked in a friendly tone.

"I am a U. S. Marshal here to see John Parker," I insisted, taking off my hat and quickly adding. "Don't be alarmed, ma'am. He knows me. I was his supervisor when he was a White House guard." She did not ask to see my identification as a federal marshal, as by that time I had none. "So far, so good," I thought.

"I will see if he is in," she replied, not quite so friendly as she had been a few seconds earlier.

"He's in," I assured her. "I saw him enter the house several minutes ago."

A reluctant John Parker slowly came to the door. "Colonel Lamon, I am surprised to see you," he stated very nervously. I was real sure he was very surprised to see me. He motioned me to come in.

"Officer Parker," I said, as I followed him into a sitting room. "I will be here just a few minutes. I want to ask you several questions." He sat down and I followed suit, sitting across from him. I set my hat and walking stick on the table between us. I let my coat fall open so that he could see that I was armed and dangerous, and that I wasn't necessarily there to bring him good tidings.

"Been asked all the questions before and have been cleared," he explained, squirming to get comfortable in his chair. He took a breath, trying to get a grip on himself, and continued. "Ain't willing to answer nothing more for you, Colonel Lamon, unless, of course, you got some kind of warrant."

"This is unofficial, Parker," I told him, "for my own personal knowledge. Tell me what happened the night in question," I continued, knowing full well he would have some inkling of what I was looking for.

He didn't say anything for several minutes, looking here and there, all around the room, but never once looking directly at me. Parker's wife had entered the room and was standing in the doorway, quite concerned as to why I was there.

"I'm as sorry as you for what happened," he finally said, actually looking remorseful. "Told Mrs. Lincoln that many times and I'll tell you that too. Been haunting me for years." He didn't go any further.

I waited him out. The first one to blink wins in a confrontation like this. I wasn't going to blink.

My gut feeling was to beat him to a pulp and exact my own personal revenge on the little frightened man sitting across from me, but for some reason I didn't. I wanted to tell him that he wasn't as sorry about Mr. Lincoln's death as I was. I knew it wouldn't make the situation any better. And it really did look like the man was hurting from the incident.

He blinked first. "I know he was your real good friend. What more can I say other than I am very sorry?" he begged, crying as he was talking. "Can't bring the president back. I've got to carry the burden of his death squarely on my shoulders. There's no one else to blame. I might as well have shot him myself. Mrs. Lincoln says it was my fault — all my fault."

This time I had nothing to say. I don't think he was looking for me to comment. In fact, he wasn't looking at me at all. His head had fallen, his eyes were looking at the floor and he was sobbing. He was indeed a broken man. His wife moved behind him and put her hand on his shoulders for comfort. My thoughts of exacting my revenge on his hide suddenly didn't matter to me.

I stood and picked up my hat and walking stick. My loaded guns remained silent. I walked out the door, down the steps and out of his life, never looking back. I didn't say good bye. I was glad that I had confronted him. At least he took responsibility even though there was no official reprimand. He was certainly being punished for his actions. I was satisfied with that, even though I was still hoping that he would rot in hell.

I returned to the Willard to pack and make my way back home. I was satisfied at least that I knew more than I did before I started my inquiries. As I wearily walked down the hall to my room, I pulled out the key. There was a small sealed envelope tacked to my door with "W. H. Lamon" written on the front. It was curious, as I had not told anyone I was going to be in Washington.

I entered the room and tore open the message. It was handwritten. The writing was not familiar to me. All it said was "Lamon. If you know what is good for you, you will stop your investigation immediately. You do not want to know what really happened."

Epilogue

Ward Hill Lamon did write a book about his friend entitled "The Life of Abraham Lincoln: From His Birth to His Inauguration as President." It was published in 1872.*

The book was highly criticized, especially by Robert Todd Lincoln, who bought most of the copies and destroyed them. He argued that Lamon revealed secrets that were damaging to Mrs. Lincoln and their family, especially information concerning Anne Rutledge.

The *Chicago Tribune* offered what might have been the most interesting critique of Lamon's book saying, "Even if every word of it were true, no excuse can palliate the atrocity of its publication."

While Lamon thought the book was a good representation of the man who was his friend, he also admitted that is was written at a time when the country "demanded the life not of a man, but of a God." Lamon said the book stated things that the public did not want to hear about its hero.

Lamon was so distraught over the criticism that he abandoned plans to write a second book. Many people thought Lamon was probably in the best position of anyone to write about Abraham Lincoln's term as President.

In his later years, Lamon did in fact reconnect with both his wife, Sally, and his daughter, Dolly. And his path crossed several more times with Mollie Pultz. He also returned quite often to visit his family in Mill Creek, which by 1879 had been renamed Bunker Hill.

Ward Hill Lamon died in Martinsburg, West Virginia on May 7, 1893. He and his daughter, Dolly, are buried in Gerrardstown, West Virginia, just a few miles from the cabin where he grew up.

*In 1999, the University of Nebraska Press reprinted the 547 page "Life of Abraham Lincoln: From His Birth to His Inauguration as President," by Ward H. Lamon. (ISBN 0-8032-7985X)

Lamon Grave — Gerrardstown, West Virginia
Gerrardstown Presbyterian Cemetery

Acknowledgments

This work of historical fiction could not have been possible without the help of many people, including: Janita Giles and Margaret LeFevre, who alerted me that the cabin where Ward Hill Lamon lived still existed near Bunker Hill. John Lamon was Mrs. LeFevre's husband's grandfather and a brother to Ward Hill Lamon's grandfather.

I would like to thank Sam Billmeyer of D. L. Morgan, Jr. Excavating for allowing me to take photographs on private property of Ward Hill Lamon's cabin.

My pursuit of this story was enhanced greatly by the discovery of the doctoral thesis of Lavern Marshall Hamand written in 1949 for the University of Illinois. His thesis was titled "Ward Hill Lamon: Lincoln's Particular Friend". I am also grateful to the family of Dr. Lavern Marshall Hamand and in particular to his daughter, Dr. Wendy Hamand Venet, professor at Georgia State University, for the family's encouragement in this fictional work.

Thanks to John Hoffmann at the University of Illinois Library for pointing me to the Danville (IL) Public Library to locate that thesis, and to Roberta Allen at that institution for helping me acquire a copy of the Hamand thesis.

I am very grateful to Dan Ostendorf and his family for helping me to locate and use three wonderful drawings of Ward Hill Lamon with Mr. Lincoln, drawn by the late Lloyd Ostendorf. And to the Library of Congress for the Alexander Gardner photograph taken at McClellan's headquarters at the Grove farm in Sharpsburg, Maryland.

Thanks to the excellent help I received in my research at the Abraham Lincoln Library in Springfield, Illinois from Dennis Suttles, Debbie Hamm and Cheryl

Schnirring. And to Alan Woodrum who is working to keep the Lamon family history alive at the Lamon House in Danville, Illinois.

Special thanks also goes to Don Woods of the Berkeley County Historical Society for research assistance, to Charles Crawford of Crawford Imaging for providing the photo scans, to Denise Walker for her excellent photograph of the author, and to Richard C. Guy for the great cover artwork.

I am very blessed by the support of my family and friends. I especially want to thank those who encouraged and nudged me along as I wrote this book, including but not limited to my daughter, Kelli Ordakowski, Doug Perks, Paulette Sprinkle, Jim Teague, my webmaster Jackie Sanders, Judy Reed, Jack Snyder, and the great staff of the Old Charles Town Library.

I appreciate greatly the professional help and support I get regularly from Michelle, John and all the great staff at my publisher, Infinity Publishing, of West Conshohocken, Pennsylvania.

Thanks to my great, new found editor, Melanie Rigney, who realized early on that although I broke all the rules of writing a novel, I perhaps knew something of what I was doing due to the success of "The Perfect Steel Trap Harpers Ferry 1859". Thanks for agreeing to work with me in spite of myself. Mel, your extra pushes were both needed and appreciated.

Lastly, I am still very grateful to my mentor and teacher, Rebecca Boreczky, for inspiring me in her publishing class at Westminster High School in Maryland in 2005, to get off my duff and become a published author. I know she is very proud of my accomplishments to date.

Coming Soon

The author's next historical novel "Catesby - Eyewitness to the Civil War" is the remarkable journey of the real slave of Colonel Lewis Washington, great grand nephew of George Washington. Follow this intriguing character through the emotional saga of his fight to free himself from the bonds of slavery, and the trials that he endured along the way. The book should be out by early 2008.

Photo by Denise Barnes Walker

Bob O'Connor

I was born in Dixon, Illinois where my Mom still lives. I work for both the Jefferson County CVB and the City of Charles Town in tourism.

My interests include traveling, reading, writing, photography and spending time with my grandkids.

I am available to make presentations and to do book signings on a regular basis.

I appreciate hearing from those who read my books. To contact me, check out my website at www.boboconnorbooks.com .